MRS CLAUS AND HER CHRISTMAS ADVENTURES

Read Aloud Stories for Children about Mrs Claus and Santa, 3 in 1 kids story bundle (ages 4-8)

CAROL ANNE CARTER

Hope Books

Mrs Claus and the Christmas Adventure

HOW MRS CLAUS SAVES CHRISTMAS AND HAS AN AMAZING ADVENTURE WITHOUT SANTA: A CHILDREN'S STORY FOR AGES 4-8

Christmas Eve At The North Pole

It was a cold and snowy Christmas Eve. A full moon shone down on Santa's workshop. But the lights of the workshop were all out. The doors were closed and locked. And it would remain that way for several months.

Nearby there was a snug little house that shone with many lights. Out in the yard, small shapes were moving about with heavy bags on their shoulders.

"Make sure you tie up the bags tightly," Santa Claus instructed the elves. "We don't want any of the presents to fall out of the sleigh!"

It was Christmas Eve! They'd been working hard for many weeks and this night marked the end of their yearly duties.

All the children's gifts were finished, all wrapped in colorful paper and tied up with red, gold and silver ribbons. It was time for Santa to deliver the presents to children all around the world.

Mrs. Claus came to the door, wearing a big white apron over her sparkly silver snowsuit. Inside, Christmas music was playing.

"I wish it could be Christmas everyday," thought Mrs. Claus. "But then again, maybe not. Poor Santa starts every Christmas skinny and gets chubbier as the night goes on. He gets such indigestion, and I am all out of air freshener!"

"What marvels you are my dears! When you finish loading the sleigh," she told the elves, "come back inside and have some hot chocolate and cookies!"

The elves grinned happily. It was a very cold night, with snow lying thick on the ground. The hot chocolate would warm their hands and the cookies fill their tummies.

"A mug of hot chocolate for you too, my dear?" said Mrs. Claus.

"Yes, please!" replied Santa. "After all, I'll have been round the world before I get my next drink."

Mrs. Claus looked right at him. 'That's *not* what the reindeer tell me,' she said, with a wink of her eye.

The sleigh was packed to bursting with presents! The sacks were piled high, and the reindeer were pawing at the ground, eager to be on their way.

Imagine the best toy shop you've ever visited. Imagine all the toys in that shop piled up in one huge mountain. That's how big the pile of sacks was in the back of Santa's sleigh.

The sacks were full of cuddly toys and books and trains. There were dolls and bicycles and snowboards, cars that tooted and cars that didn't. There were gadgets that lit up, and toys that made so much noise that poor grandmas across the world would be putting their hands over their ears on Christmas morning.

There was every toy you can imagine and a few that you probably can't!

Santa Is On His Way

After drinking his hot chocolate, Santa changed out of his slippers and pulled on his warm red boots. He slipped his arms into his thick red jacket, lined with fluffy white fur, pulling the collar tightly about his neck. He buttoned up each one of the shiny golden buttons with care.

Finally, he put on his red hat, pulling it down over his ears to keep them warm.

"I'll be back soon," Santa said to Mrs. Claus and gave her a warm kiss on the cheek. "We can leave for vacation right after I get home!"

Every year, on Christmas Day, Santa and Mrs. Claus went on vacation. This year, they were going to the beach! Mrs. Claus was looking forward to it. She imagined herself on a sandy beach, with drinks, decorated with tiny umbrellas, and rubbing sun screen into her nose.

"Have a safe trip," Mrs. Claus called out. "Try not to eat too many cookies this year! And stay clear of the mince pies! Those buttons get tighter every year when you get back."

The reindeers pulling the sleigh were getting impatient, especially Rudolph! He was so excited. His nose was already bright red, ready to light the way through the night sky.

It was a lovely scene. The elves gathered around to wave goodbye to Santa. Mrs. Claus was smiling, mainly because it was Christmas, but partly because she would have their home to herself for the night.

She could put her feet up, watch a Christmas movie and check the vacation bags to make sure she had got everything, especially the sun screen! Atop the sleigh, Santa sat proudly, whilst the reindeer pawed the ground excitedly.

"Goodbye, Santa," cried the elves. "See you later!"

"Goodbye, my dear," cried Mrs. Claus. "I'll be ready when you return!"

Holding on to the reins, Santa gave a shout and the reindeer began to run down the ski way. The sleigh glided across the snow, then flew up into the sky. Santa was on his way to make Christmas a wonderful time for children all over the world.

The Terrible Discovery

Meanwhile, Mrs. Claus waved goodbye to the elves who walked home to their elf village. She went back inside the house and started to choose which Christmas movie she was going to watch. She loved the old black and white ones, but some of the new ones were quite fun too.

There were still bits of wrapping paper and ribbons on the floor. Mrs Claus rolled all the left-over ribbons into a ball. She put them away so they could be used again next Christmas. They didn't have a lot of wrapping paper left, though. There were so many gifts this year, they almost didn't finish packing all of them!

Finally, she finally sat down on her rocking chair beside the fire. She leaned over to reach for the TV remote control. And that's when she saw them.

There, beside her chair were three presents! "Goodness me!" gasped Mrs. Claus. "I forgot to put those three presents into the sacks! I tell you," she said to her coffee mug, "I'm getting as forgetful as…!" but she couldn't remember what she'd been about to say.

There was a big gift for a little girl called Freja who lives in Sweden. There was a box for a boy called Mukami in Africa. And there was a red and white spotted package for a pair of twins, Ethan and Olivia, who live in Canada.

Mrs Claus was worried. "This simply won't do", she said. "Something must be done!"

Santa had only just left on the magic sleigh with every single one of the reindeer. How could she deliver the presents without a sleigh or any reindeer? How could she fly so far in just one night? She sat back down in her rocking chair and tried to think of a plan.

Mrs. Claus couldn't bear to think of any boys and girls being disappointed on Christmas morning. She imagined the looks on their faces as they searched in vain for Santa's gift. They would wonder what more they could possibly have done to deserve a present.

Suddenly an idea came into her head. "I know what to do," Mrs. Claus said, "but I'll need some help".

She stood up. She had a plan, but she had to act fast.

4

Helpful Friends

Mrs. Claus changed out of her sparkling silver shoes and pulled on some warm socks and a pair of sturdy red boots.

Wrapping up warm in a silver snowsuit with a white fur collar, she put the children's presents in a small sack she found, slung it over her shoulder and headed out of the front door.

She strode along the street, under the twinkling lights with their colored stars and to a happy looking little cottage.

Mrs. Claus was facing the front door of her neighbor, the Tooth Fairy. She knocked loudly, hoping the Fairy would be home. She was in luck. The living room lights flashed on and a very sleepy Tooth Fairy opened the door.

"Happy Christmas Eve," yawned the Tooth Fairy. "What's the matter, Mrs. Claus? Is something wrong? Chewed on a hard toffee?" The tooth fairy looked hopeful.

"Oh! I'm sorry to have woken you," replied Mrs. Claus.

"Something terrible has happened and I need your help to fix it!"

"Have your false teeth fallen out? I've got some glue somewhere." The tooth fairy did sometimes jump to crazy conclusions.

When Mrs Claus explained the problem, the Tooth Fairy's eyes were suddenly wide open. It would never do to disappoint the children. And on Christmas Day, no less!

The Tooth Fairy went to the mantle on top of her fireplace. She opened a wooden box with a star and tooth motif and peered inside. Taking out a small jar from inside and handed it to Mrs Claus.

"I still have a bit of fairy dust left. It can take you some of the way, but it may not be quite enough for the whole trip!"

"I'm sure I'll think of something," said Mrs. Claus. "But even if I have fairy dust, where will I sprinkle it? I'll have to ride something because I have these presents with me."

They searched all through the Tooth Fairy's house. The Tooth Fairy pulled out her sledge, then her skis, then her bicycle. But none of them were any good. The problem was, of course, that fairies are rather small, and Mrs. Claus wasn't.

They were running out of ideas and the clock was ticking! Finally, Mrs. Claus decided to call the elves for help. There was much chattering at the other end of the phone. Then there was silence, followed by a loud cheer.

"The elves said they have found something," Mrs. Claus said when she put down the telephone. "They are bringing it over right now."

One of the elves had indeed found something. It was an old battered snowboard. A proper sized one. He remembered when Mrs Claus herself had come second in the North Pole Snowboarding championships on this very board.

It had once been Mrs Claus's prize possession, but she'd long since lost all her confidence and hadn't ridden it. The snowboard had long since been discarded in a corner, gathering dust.

The board didn't look like much, it had chipped paint and the colors were faded. Yet underneath everything, it was a prize-winning snowboard.

The elf picked it up. He couldn't wait to show it to Mrs. Claus. He decided to run all the way from the elf village to Santa's house. Then a bright idea came to him. It was snowing, and this was a snowboard. Why not try it out, just to see if the old board still had the magic touch?

He stepped on to the board and set off. Sure enough, the board made it feel as if he was gliding along effortlessly. It might not look in the best of shape, but it did a brilliant job. He only hoped that Mrs. Claus would remember how to ride it, like she once did.

As he glided down the path to the Claus's house, Mrs. Claus opened the door. She was impatient to see what the elves had found for her.

As soon as she saw the elf on the board, Mrs Claus began to clap excitedly. "That will work beautifully," she cried. With the board in hand, she could hardly wait to set out to deliver the presents.

5

Mrs Claus To The Rescue!

The Tooth Fairy was sprinkling fairy dust onto the snowboard while the elf carefully strapped the gifts to the front, using dental floss he'd found in the Tooth Fairy's cabin.

The Tooth Fairy handed the small jar of fairy dust to Mrs. Claus, who tucked it carefully into a pocket.

"Thank you so much for your help," Mrs. Claus said.

"Good luck, Mrs. Claus," she replied.

"But remember, you must be careful not to run out of fairy dust. It's all in your 'elf and safety' manual" added the Tooth Fairy. "Take care and stay safe!"

Before Mrs. Claus left, one of the elves gave her a small golden pouch.

"It's a magic pouch and it is for emergencies!" said the elf. "The pouch will give what you need, when you need it."

"Thank you! Sounds very useful!" Mrs. Claus nodded, snapping her snow goggles over her eyes and clipping her boots into the snowboard.

She pointed the board down the runaway Santa used and toward Sweden. She was ready, this was it.

Mrs C's heart thumped in her chest, hoping against hope that she would remember her magnificent moves. She might have come second and lost to Snozzle all those years ago, but tonight would show that she'd still got it. Most importantly, the children were counting on her and she refused to let them down.

The moon was shining brightly, lighting her way. She leant forward and the board started sliding downward. There was no going back now.

The wind whistled in her ears and the cold stung her face. Yes! This is where she belonged. It had been too long since she had been on her fantastic board. Why had she let it just chip and fade in a corner.?

It didn't matter that she hadn't won, she loved this. She started twisting and turning down the slope, her body on autopilot, remembering how to move.

The first jump was coming up. This was the real test to see whether she would be able to deliver all those presents.

WHOOSH!! As she took off, the sky blazed with beautiful colors. Swathes of green ran across it, like a river of light running through the heavens. "The northern lights!" cried Mrs. Claus in delight. She twisted and turned on the snowboard, remembering long-forgotten moves. Soon she was gliding along the beautiful green lights, up and down, in waves across the night sky.

It felt wonderful to be on her old board again. Mrs C's memories of that championship run came flooding back. Using her expert snowboarding skills (not to mention a sprinkling of fairy dust) she knew she would make it to Sweden in no time.

It was pretty chilly up in the frosty winter air. Mrs. Claus pulled the red hat down over her ears to keep them warm.

As she passed some clouds, an airplane appeared. For a while she glided along next to the plane. A little boy waved excitedly to her out of his window, rubbing his eyes before falling back to sleep and imagining that it was all just a dream.

Mrs. Claus and the snowboard glided high over vast snowy fields, touching down occasionally to perfect some of her old favorite tricks on the mountain sides. It was peaceful and quiet, except for the sound of the board cutting through the freshly laid snow.

She flew over great forests and seas. She had no company but the stars.

Soon, she could see lights ahead. They were coming from the buildings in a city. She was in Sweden! No time for tricks now, she had a present to deliver and couldn't waste any time!

Something in the middle of the town square caught her eye. She slowed the snowboard down so she could have a better look.

"Wow!" said Mrs. Claus. There was a giant straw goat, almost bigger than her house back in the North Pole! It had a red noose, a red bridle and even red shoes. The top of the goat's head was heaped with fallen snow, but Mrs. Claus could still see its merry black eyes looking back at her.

They didn't have straw goats in the North Pole. In fact, they didn't have goats at all. "What a lovely idea", she said out loud to no-one in particular.

She went on her way, noticing that all the houses had small lights that swirled and swayed with the wind.

"I wonder why," she thought, but she soon found out.

The swaying lights were small white candles that stood in every window.

Mrs. Claus decided that the people living in Sweden were very thoughtful. The candles just gave enough light for Santa to deliver his presents in the middle of the night!

Inside each house, she could see the twinkling stars coming from their Christmas trees, lighting up the room. Everyone was asleep. She wanted to hurry, but she had to be careful. She knew that she had to be very quiet!

The first present was addressed to a little girl named Freja who lived on Stor Sjögata (that's Swedish for Big Lake Street).

She flew over the rooftops, along a tree lined track until she saw a wooden cabin with smoke drifting up and out of its chimney. The cabin sat beside a frozen lake, surrounded by tall pine trees. It was a beautiful scene.

This was Freja's home. It was time for Mrs Claus to deliver her first present.

6

The Golden Pouch

Mrs. Claus landed softly on the snow. Stepping off the snowboard, her boots crushed the snow with a soft crunching sound. She walked carefully up to the front of the house. She gently tried the handle. The front door was locked.

She wondered how she would get inside. "Santa lands his sleigh on the roof so he can go down the chimney," thought Mrs. Claus. "I don't want to get dirty from all the ash! More importantly, I don't want a burned bottom. Is there another way to get in?"

She walked around the back of the house. There was a kitchen door. Again, she tried the handle but it too was locked. She sighed. This was harder than she'd imagined.

Suddenly she remembered the golden pouch from the elf.

She took out the pouch from her pocket and slowly opened it.

Inside was a small golden key.

"I wonder if this key will work," she thought.

She slid the key into the key hole of the kitchen door and turned it.

CLICK!

It worked! The golden pouch had given her a magic key to open any door.

As she stepped inside, she heard a soft, low growl. Turning her head, Mrs. Claus gasped as she saw the biggest dog she had ever seen! It was big and fluffy. It had large brown eyes and a soft brown tail. It would have been cute, if only it hadn't been growling at her!

She didn't want to wake Freja or her parents up. So, Mrs. Claus grabbed the golden pouch once more.

"Perhaps there is something here for growling dogs," she wished.

The pouch didn't disappoint her. There inside, waiting for her, was a dog biscuit. She quickly tossed the biscuit to the other end of the room. The dog turned and ran to get it while Mrs. Claus hurriedly tiptoed into the living room.

"Happy Christmas," she said.

"Woof," thanked the dog.

She stopped and looked for a while. This was one of the nicest living rooms she had ever seen. There was a big fir tree, covered with shining Christmas baubles. There were small twinkling lights around it. And best of all, there was a plate of mince pies and a glass of milk on the table beside the tree.

"I think it's time for a little snack! I'm rather tired after snowboarding all the way from the North Pole," she whispered as she sat down to eat. By this time, the dog came sniffing back. It had smelled the pies and it wasn't growling anymore. Mrs. Claus shared her pie with the dog and gave it a gentle pat on the head.

Then, she gently placed Freja's gift under tree, right next to the other presents.

"I hope Freja enjoys her new ski boots," smiled Mrs. Claus. She stopped for a moment and gave a little sigh. She was loving her adventure. It made her so happy to be giving the children gifts that would bring smiles to their faces on Christmas morning. "This is how Santa must feel every time he gives someone a present. How marvellous!"

But she didn't stop for long. It was time to deliver the rest of the presents.

7

A Crash Landing

Mrs. Claus went back outside and jumped back on the snowboard. She remembered the tooth fairy's warning, but she hoped that she had enough fairy dust for one more trip.

Pulling the fairy dust from her pocket, she tapped gently once, then twice, until a few sparkles of fairy dust fell onto the snowboard. All at once the snowboard began to tug away from the snow. It was ready for the next stage of their journey.

She made sure that the other presents were still safely tied on to the snowboard. "Up and away", she cried. Quickly rising into the air, Mrs. Claus looked down on the frozen lake beside Freja's house. "Sweden is rather lovely" she thought, as she rose into the cold night sky.

But Mrs. Claus' adventure had only just begun. As she reached the edge of the town, the snowboard started wiggle under her. The board wobbled and tipped. The two remaining presents almost fell right off! Mrs. Claus was going to crash!

The snowboard was vibrating hard as it descended to the ground

BUMP!

CRACK!

Mrs Claus tumbled off into a snow bank. Slowly, she stood up and brushed the snow off. Oh dear, that had been some crash. Was she alright? Arms, legs, head, all OK. Yes, it seemed that nothing was broken.

It was then that she looked down at the board. There was a huge crack running right down the middle. She wasn't hurt, but the board was broken. Worse still, she was stuck in the middle of nowhere, in Sweden!

Tears rolled down Mrs Claus's face. She knew it was silly to get so upset about her old board. She hadn't even looked at it for years but gliding along on the snow had brought back so many happy memories.

"This poor snowboard has had enough. It's travelled across several countries already, but we have so much further to travel. How am I going to deliver the presents if I can't fly?" she wondered.

"Oh no, don't be sad" a low voice said from nearby. "I can help you with that."

Mrs. Claus turned around and saw a pair of big brown eyes in the gloom. At the edge of the trees, there was a rounded head looking at her.

"Hello there and happy Christmas Eve," said a Moose. "Are you Santa?"

"Oh, no!" she sniffed. "But I am his wife."

Mrs. Claus told the story of her predicament to the moose. She was so happy when the moose said that he was happy to help. "But, I'm afraid I can't fly", he said as his shoulders drooped a little. "No problemo!" said Mrs Claus, "watch what happens when I use a bit of fairy dust".

Mrs Claus remembered what the elf had told her about the pouch being a magic pouch. She opened the top and it started to stretch. Gently, she placed the presents inside the stretching pouch, followed by the pieces of her broken board. It now was much larger and the strings round he top were now straps for her to put her arm through.

"To Africa," she cried, jumping onto the moose's back. She sprinkled on some flecks of fairy dust and they were off.

Mrs Claus was exhausted after all the boarding she had done. "I really could do with a little nap, just to get my strength back," she thought as she drifted off to sleep, dreaming of her nice warm bed. She slept and dreamed as they crossed the ocean.

"Time to wake up" said the moose.

"This doesn't look like Africa" she muttered, as she rubbed her eyes, stretched and looked around her. They were on an island, in the middle of the ocean, surrounded by sea.

"I'm sorry, I really must return to my family in Sweden", said the moose, "but I've taken you half way across the ocean. I'm leaving you in safe hands. I've found someone who will take you the next step of your journey."

Out from behind a large rock, peered a curious face. It was a big brown turtle. It was a friendly face, the sort of face that you could trust. Mrs. Claus found herself telling the story of her predicament to the turtle. She was delighted when the turtle said that he could pull her all the way to the coast of Africa.

"I can ask the other turtles to help," said Mrs. Claus' new friend. "We have to swim fast so we can make it on time. Can you swim?"

Sadly, Mrs. Claus couldn't! But she remembered the small gold pouch which was now a rather large knapsack from the elf.

She opened up the pouch and saw that something rather amazing had happened.

The pouch had repaired her snowboard! Not only that it had given it a new paint job! It looked better that it had done it years. It was a bright Christmas red but with silver sparkles, just like Mrs Claus's boots. It even had her name written across it.

Mrs Claus flushed with happiness and cried out with joy, "Oh thank you!" The bag held another gift, a wake-boarding towline. Mrs Claus blinked in amazement. Santa was never going to believe here story when she got back home.

Refreshed after her nap, she was ready to test out her old, but improved, board on the clear, warm water.

"Aha," said the turtle. "What a marvellous solution to our problem!"

In the Middle Of The Ocean

Mrs Claus gingerly clipped her boots into the board and picked up the towline handle. Snowboarding and wake boarding and pretty much the same right? She hoped so!

She had already attached the turtles to the other end of the towline and had applied a sprinkle of fairy dust to each of the turtle shells.

"Are you ready?" asked the turtles. "Here we go!"

In the bright moonlight, the turtles dived down and pulled the line taught. With their big flippers, they pulled her easily. With the help of a little fairy dust, they were going very fast!

It was like flying through the air, but wetter! The sea sent sprays of water that splashed and hit Mrs. Claus' bare face and hands.

"Thank goodness for my goggles!" she thought. "And thank goodness for the turtles and thank goodness for the golden bbllubbllll!" as she rode a particularly big wave and the crest of the wave splashed in her face.

They travelled in the dark for a long time. After riding the waves for what seemed like a long time, Mrs. Claus started to feel sleepy.

'Mrs Turtle,' yawned Mrs C, 'would you be so kind as to let me rest on your shell? I've been boarding for hours and could do with a snooze.'

'Of course, you poor thing. Yes, of course. I'll make sure my shell stays above water.'

'Thank you," replied Mrs Claus. She stowed the towline in the golden knapsack with her snowboard, and curled up on the strong shell of the kind turtle.

"I wonder how Santa is doing with his other deliveries," she thought drowsily and she closed her eyes.

Mrs Claus Arrives In Africa

She awoke to a bump and the movement of the turtle making her way up the beach.

"We're here!" said the turtle. Mrs. Claus looked around but there wasn't much to see. It was very dark, but she could hear the sound of laughter and singing nearby.

It was deliciously warm. Mrs Claus took off her hat, scarf and gloves and popped them inside the golden bag.

"It's the middle of the night. Why do you think everyone is still awake?" she asked.

"In Kenya," the turtle said. "They love to celebrate. They have a big party on Christmas Eve that lasts almost until morning."

To deliver her gift without being seen, Mrs. Claus had to pass through the village quietly so she could get to the boy's home.

"I have to bring this gift to a little boy named Mukami," she whispered.

The turtle pointed to a straw hut in the distance. "That's Mukami's house," she said.

Mrs. Claus gave the turtle her thanks. She couldn't have come all this way without her!

"We must go back to our island and to our families," said the turtle. "We are also celebrating Christmas."

Carefully and as quietly as she could, Mrs. Claus slung the golden bag over her shoulder. The village looked deserted, but she could still hear the sounds of merriment just on the other side of the trees.

"That's where all the grown-ups are," she thought. "But the children must already be sleeping."

She went inside Mukami's house, stepping softly onto the earthen floor.

Mukami's family had a small plastic tree beside the window, but it had no twinkling Christmas lights. There were a few small presents under it, though, so Mrs. Claus reached into the golden bag and placed the boy's gift on the floor beside the others.

Mrs. Claus looked around her curiously. This straw hut was plainer than Freja's house in Sweden. She noticed an open book, some sheets of paper and a pencil lying on the floor. Mukami had been doing his homework before he fell asleep.

"I hope Mukami enjoys his brand new school uniform," she whispered. That's when she realised the music outside had stopped.

"Oh no!" said Mrs. Claus. "They are done with their party and all the grown-ups are coming back home!"

It would never do to be seen. The straw hut only had one room and the little boy Mukami was sleeping inside. Where could she go?

Mrs. Claus took out the golden pouch once more and this time, she pulled out a very thick and very black wool blanket.

"I'll just put this over my head and hopefully they won't see me in the corner of the house!"

She found the darkest corner and crouched. She pulled the blanket over her head and didn't make a sound.

The door opened with a little click and Mukami's parents came inside. Thankfully, they were so tired and sleepy that they didn't notice the black shape in the corner. They didn't even see that there was an extra gift under the tree!

The two grown-ups went straight to sleep. Mrs. Claus heard them say goodnight to each other and then all was quiet again.

Soon there was a gentle sound of snoring. "Whew! That was a close one," she thought.

She waited a few more minutes just to make sure that everyone was fast asleep before she took off the wool blanket and stepped back outside.

In The Jungle

'Hmm, how on earth am I going to get to Canada from here? wondered Mrs C. 'The turtles have gone to celebrate Christmas with their own families.'

She couldn't board across the ocean without some help.

She opened the jar of fairy dust. A couple of flecks of dust glimmered at the bottom. It wasn't nearly enough fairy dust to get both her *and* the snowboard airborne. Certainly not enough to take them all the way to Canada.

"What am I going to do?" she said with a whimper.

Mrs. Claus saw down on a flat rock and looked up. Through a canopy of leaves, she could see the moon.

"I wonder if Santa has problems like this when he delivers presents every year."

She decided to look into the golden sack once more. It helped her so many times on this adventure. Maybe it could help her again.

When she opened it, all she could see was coils of silvery strings. She wondered why it was there. How was she going to Canada with strings?

With a huff, Mrs. Claus stood up. She decided that she wasn't going to worry anymore. She had to find a way to out of this problem herself.

She took a step, and then another, walking deeper into the jungle.

The trees pressed close all around her. It was so quiet that she felt a little scared. She had never been to a jungle before and now she found herself in the middle of one, in the middle of the night!

There were roots and rocks on the ground so she had to step carefully if she didn't want to trip. It became hard to make her way through, with the branches and leaves on every side of her.

She heard the calls of wild animals in the distance and the sound made goosebumps rise up on her arms.

Somewhere above her, she heard a startlingly loud squawk.

11

Flapping Feathers

Mrs. Claus peered up and nearly jumped out of her skin.

There, on the branches of a big willow tree, were yellow eyes looking down at her. In fact, there were eyes on every branch. There were big eyes and small eyes. Slanted eyes and rounded eyes. They may have been many shapes, but they were all bright yellow and all looking right at her.

"Squawk! Squawk!"

The sound of flapping wings was all around her. All she could see were flapping feathers.

"Squawk, are you lost?" said a voice that sounded very old and wise.

Mrs. Claus had closed her eyes when she'd seen all those eyes staring at her, but now she opened them again. Parrots! There were hundreds of them and they were all perched around her.

"Oh, my!" exclaimed Mrs. Claus. "How many parrots are here around me?"

"We are a parliament of parrots," said the biggest and most colorful of them all. "I am their leader, Blue Feather. How can we help you? You look rather lost."

The rest of the parliament of parrots squawked loudly and meaninglessly, talking over the top of each other to get their voices heard.

Mrs. Claus' worry vanished. Here, in this frightening and dark place were friends, even though they were somewhat loud. And messy, she thought, as she carefully wiped a dollop of droppings from her shoulder!

She told them about her problem. She began the story with how the presents had been left behind. She told them how she'd come to be stranded in Africa, while the twins were in Canada waiting for their presents.

"Squawk," said the chief Blue Feather again. "I saw you come ashore with the turtles and then watched them leave again. Don't worry. We'll all help you. But how?"

Blue Feather stopped and thought for a moment.

Mrs Claus stopped and thought for a moment. Then, inspiration struck!

"Blue Feather, could you assemble your parliament? I have an idea…"

12

Across The Sea

It was time to say goodbye to Africa. Mrs Claus pulled on her warm hat, scarf and gloves, sad to leave the warmth and beauty of the African jungle.

Blue Feather told each of the other parrots to take the string and cut it to the same length. Then, the parrots wrapped it under the snowboard. They took the ends of each string and tied them to their claws.

"You want us to carry you? Of course!" said the parrot.

And so it was that in the middle of the night, deep in the heart of the African jungle, a snowboard tied to a hundred parrots flew high into the air and headed for Canada!

Mrs Claus snapped her goggles over her eyes and spread the last remaining flecks of fairy dust on the snowboard. Soon they were speeding across the sky faster than a jumbo jet.

"Off we go," cried the Blue Feather who was at the front of

the group. He flapped his wings and all the other parrots followed. Under the light of the full moon, they found their way easily.

If anyone had decided to look up, it was an extraordinary sight to see. The moon was big and bright, casting a silhouette over hundreds of parrots. There was Mrs. Claus clipped into her snowboard.

She flew with perfect balance, holding onto the nearest strings and the golden sack (now much smaller) containing the last present for the twins in Canada.

As they flew across Africa, Mrs. Claus could see the long necks of the giraffes as they reached for the highest leaves of the trees. She saw lions chasing a hyena across the savannah. Then she saw the ocean, dark and vast and calm, the rays of the moon glinting on the water.

With the soothing sounds of the parrot's wings beating as one, Mrs. Claus was feeling sleepy again, but she didn't dare go to sleep this time. She might tumble right off the board and fall all the way down into the ocean below!

They flew higher and higher, and soon they were soaring above the clouds. There was no time to waste, they must reach Canada and find the twins home.

On they flew, over the top of a noisy raging waterfall. On over a great lake that reflected the moon in its waters. They soared over vast mountain ranges and huge rivers.

At last they saw the lights of a city. It was the home of the twins, straight ahead!

13

The Last Present

The parrots began their descent. It was a bright night and Mrs Claus could see right across the rooftops of the city.

There were tall buildings, street lamps and the lights of Christmas trees twinkling at windows. She could see that snow covered the whole city. It looked like a winter wonderland.

She realized that she would have to be very careful here. She had to be smart to deliver the last present without being seen!

Blue Feather squawked a question to a passing lark.

"Where can we find Ethan and Olivia's home?"

The lark pointed the way and the parrots flew down. Canadian larks are known for their intelligence, and excellent sense of direction.

But instead of landing on the ground, Mrs. Claus was surprised to find herself landing on the roof of one of the tall buildings.

"Ethan and Olivia live in Apartment 107, on the 10th floor," said Blue Feather.

Mrs. Claus began to wonder how she could deliver their present. She couldn't take the elevator. She couldn't just walk down the hallway. She couldn't be seen, so how could she get into an apartment on the 10th floor of a building?

Once more, she opened the magic pouch but, to her great disappointment, the bag was now empty, apart from the present for the twins. There was nothing for it. She would have to find a way in.

"An apartment has no chimney," she thought. "I can't fly through the window because I have so little fairy dust." For the second time that night, Mrs Claus had a fantastic plan. She said goodbye and thank you to the parrots.

"I couldn't have done it without your help," she said. The parrots nodded and flew back into the night sky. It was time for them to return to the jungle.

Mrs. Claus left her snowboard perched on the roof. Clutching the last present, she tiptoed quietly down the fire escape.

When she passed Ethan and Olivia's apartment, she gave a sigh. She could see the twins sleeping inside their bedroom. It would have been so easy to climb through the window, but Olivia's bed was underneath the window and she dare not risk waking them up.

Down and down she went until she reached the ground floor. Then down another flight of stairs that led to the basement. It was filled with empty garbage bins.

Mrs. Claus was going to climb all the way back up to the 10th floor using the garbage chute!

14

A Tight Fit

To Mrs Claus's horror, the garbage chute was not very clean. It smelled of garlic and banana peel. Lumps of newspaper were bundled up, and there were a lot of pizza boxes.

Inside some of them she could smell half eaten Pepperoni slices. She edged herself up the chute, one inch at time. After just a few feet, the rubbish chute got a little tighter as it went around a bend. Mrs. Claus was stuck!

"Uh-oh," she said.

She began to wiggle, twist and squirm. It was no good, her bottom was well and truly stuck in the chute.

"If I don't get out of this, I will be here until the New Year," said Mrs. Claus.

She wriggled and twisted and pushed again. She turned and struggled and rotated. She could go down, but not up.

Suddenly, from up above, she saw a small light. Then she

heard a rumbling. "Uh-Oh" she thought. She wasn't wrong. In a second, she was covered with tissues and dust and jars. Somebody was having a clear out.

"It's the middle of the night," she thought to herself, removing a jar of cream from her head. Then she had an idea.

She opened the jar, gave a sniff, and recoiled. It was some seriously weird-smelling cream. "The twins' presents are more important than the way I smell," she said to herself.

She put her hand into the jar, scooped out a handful of the smelly stuff, and spread it around the walls of the chute.

By pushing and wiggling, she discovered she could move up an inch. Mrs Claus repeated the process twice more, and suddenly she was free. The chute opened up and she could continue her journey.

"Thanks, jar of cream," she said, "I take back all I said about you being smelly." Then she threw it down the chute behind her. As it fell she saw the label. 'Happy Hemorrhoids – relief from Piles' it said. "Ugh"! The jar had contained bottom cream.

Soon, she had wiggled enough to see that she was just outside the rubbish door of Apartment 107 on the 10th floor.

She quietly opened the door and squeezed herself through it. She looked around and sighed in relief. No dogs this time. She listened carefully and could hear snores coming from another room. Hurrah! It sounded as if they were all asleep.

Mrs. Claus crept into the living room and saw the Christmas tree. The tree was decorated with red ribbons and twinkling lights. She placed the twins present beside the rest. When she looked around, she saw that the living room was full of pictures of the twins.

"I do hope they enjoy their toy dinosaurs!" thought Mrs. Claus.

After all that she had been through that night, Mrs. Claus took a sip out of the eggnog that the twins had left on the table beside the tree. She nibbled one or two of the biscuits as well.

"I did it!" she thought to herself. "I made all the deliveries. Now, all the children will have a happy Christmas morning!"

She left the house the same way she went in. It seemed to have taken ages to climb all the way up here, but it took just seconds as she slid down the garbage chute.

Mrs Claus landed with a bump on the pile of garbage, her fall cushioned by the mostly empty pizza boxes. As she surfaced from the garbage mountain, she moved her hand upwards to her head.

"Oh my, oh dear," she said, as she gingerly removed a slightly mouldy slice of pepperoni pizza stuck to the top of her head.

She picked herself up and brushed herself down. Then she began the long climb up the fire escape stairs, to return to her snowboard.

Despite everything, she had a little skip in her step. She'd done it! She'd delivered every single present.

15

Finding The Way Home

All this time, Mrs. Claus had only been thinking about getting the gifts to the children. She didn't even bother to think of how she was going back to the North Pole! But now, dawn was near.

She was still wearing her sparkling silver snowsuit. And she was stuck on the roof, and very far from her home in the North Pole.

"How will I get home?" wondered Mrs. Claus.

There were no friendly animals nearby. She had no more fairy dust. And the golden pouch (now back to its original size) seemed to be out of useful gifts for her.

The pouch seemed to hear what she thinking. A shrill whistle sounded from inside it. Curious, Mrs. Claus opened the pouch again.

"Glow sticks!" she cried. "And a whistle!"

She knew that she needed all those things to attract the notice of somebody. But who?

Suddenly, she heard the sound of bells. Then the sound of a jolly laugh.

"Ho! Ho! Ho! "

It was Santa and his sleigh. As she turned, she could see him clearly. He was on the roof of the building, just two streets away!

Quick as a flash, Mrs. Claus lit up the glow sticks. They glowed green and bright in the moonlit sky. Then she placed the whistle to her lips and blew.

Santa turned around at the sound. His mouth fell open as he saw his wife standing on the roof of an apartment building with a whistle in her mouth and waving her arms.

In a trice, Santa and the sleigh were on the rooftop with Mrs Claus. Too quick, in fact, for him to hide the large mince pie in his hand.

"My dear, what on earth are you doing here?" sputtered Santa in astonishment, spraying pastry crumbs over her and the sleigh.

"A few things got left behind, back at home, my love," Mrs. Claus said as she climbed in to sit beside Santa on the sleigh. Santa had delivered all his presents and every sack lay empty. The reindeer looked tired, but happy.

"Tell me all about what happened. Where did you go and what did you do?" asked Santa.

"Oh, this and that," replied Mrs. Claus. "It will take such a long time to tell you my story. I will still be talking when we get back home!"

Santa smiled at his wife. Her eyes were sparkling and her cheeks were glowing red in the moonlight. He had never seen Mrs. Claus looking quite so tired or quite so happy.

"I'll tell you about my adventures later," yawned Mrs. Claus. "But for now, I am just relieved that all the presents have been delivered. And when I say all the presents, I mean every last one!"

The gentle strides of the reindeers made were comforting. It was so very cosy in the sleigh and this time Mrs. Claus didn't have to be afraid that she was going to fall off! The snowboard was tucked in at the back. It too looked proud of its part in their adventure. If, that is, a snowboard can look proud.

"Please remind me to thank the elves for finding my old snowboard," she said before she dozed off. "I will thank the elves and the Tooth Fairy with all my heart. Without them, I wouldn't have been able to deliver the presents.'

With that, her head fell on her chest and she finally closed her eyes. Santa chuckled softy as he opened the small golden pouch on her lap. Inside, he found a thick black woollen blanket.

"Have a nice nap, Mrs. Claus," whispered Santa. "You deserve it!

Mrs. Claus heard him and she smiled. She was tired, but a part of her wished that Santa Claus would forget a few more presents next year.

"But next time, I will make sure that I have enough fairy dust," was her last thought as she drifted into a well-deserved sleep.

The moon moved to the edge of the sky to make room for the sun. Christmas Eve was over, and now it was Christmas morning.

All the children in the world would soon be waking up soon to find their presents from Santa, or from his adventurous wife, Mrs. Claus!

THE END

Mrs Claus and the Pirate Captain

A CHILDREN'S CHRISTMAS ADVENTURE STORY ABOUT SANTA AND HIS WIFE : A CHILDREN'S STORY FOR AGES 4-8

1

Santa's Brilliant Idea

It was Christmas Eve at the North Pole. All the reindeer were ready.

Dasher, Dancer, Prancer and their friends looked magnificent. But so did Leena, Inara, Anneli and Ansa, Astro, Leaky, Thomas and Tapio.

To be fair, Astro was pawing the ground gently, looking a little uncomfortable. But there was nothing unusual in that.

And as for Leaky? Well, he was … leaky. Little yellow polka dots in the snow told Mrs Claus where he had been.

She noticed that her husband's reindeer still looked down their noses at her own sleigh pulling reindeer. But that was understandable. After all, they had been doing the job for centuries. Her own reindeer were on their first ever venture.

Behind the splendid animals, their antlers glittering in the midnight moon, stood two sleighs. And what magnificent sleighs they were. Santa had said, no insisted, that if Mrs Claus was to become an official present deliverer this Christmas, then she had to look the part. And so did her sleigh. They both did.

Her own red, fluffy coat was trimmed in white, a matching belt sparkled with diamonds and her boots were long and shiny. Of course, she had no beard… but the white woollen scarf tied around her neck was at least as spectacular as her husband's mane.

The matching gold and red sleighs, lights blinking like shining eyes, piled high with presents of all shapes and sizes, filled her with excitement. The elves had done a good job, there was no doubt about that.

Last year, Mrs Claus had only helped because it was an emergency. Santa, forgetful old fool that he was, had left behind some important gifts. And that had led to Santa's *BRILLIANT IDEA*.

You see, Santa was getting on a bit. There were plenty of years left in the old tubs, but everyone can do with a hand, especially if they have a particularly busy night ahead.

It was the special deliveries that caused the problems. Sometimes a mum, dad or sister - even a brother, had to spend a year working on some important scientific study or just travel the world.

As Santa always said, just because a boy or a girl lived hundreds of miles from anybody else, it didn't mean that they were less entitled to a gift at Christmas. (As long, of course, as their behaviour deserved it). The problem was that having to detour, to Antarctica or find some tents in the Sahara, took a while. And the reindeer were liable to get grumpy, especially that Prancer.

Take the incident a couple of years ago. They'd been running so late, some children in Hawaii (one of his last stops) were waking up by the time he popped down their air conditioning unit.

Oh, if only the manufacturers would make those a bit bigger, he was getting on, and so was his tum. Admittedly, his fondness for mince pies didn't help. You should try getting down an outside flue after a glass or eighty million of brandy!

So Mr and Mrs Claus had had a chat. Mrs Claus had suggested that she could take on 'the specials', leaving more time for Santa to deliver to the towns and villages and cities of the world. Here now, in front of her was the result. And it was magnificent.

2

Mrs Claus Takes Off

Mrs Claus cast one final look at the sleigh, waved to her helper elves already on board and admired her reindeer waiting eagerly on the sharp white snow...or, in Leaky's case, the slightly yellow snow.

'Let's go, then dear.' Santa was already aboard his own sleigh. His face was shining with excitement. He was the same every Christmas. He might be old, but he was still a boy at heart.

Mrs Claus clambered aboard and did her final safety check. Seat belts – check; present delivery system – check; automated carrot dispenser – check. Although she suspected the Reindeer would get enough treats not to need that.

'Prepare for take-off...' she instructed. 'Flight crew to their seats.' The elves belted themselves in and they headed for the ski way.

'Flight two oh one eight, special deliveries, ready for take-off,' she instructed to the ice tower overlooking the ski way.

Ahead of her Santa's sleigh was already airborne. In front of her she could see the reindeer straining at their reins; all apart from Astro who seemed a little bit distracted. Leaky was living up to his name, and Mrs Claus hoped he wouldn't melt the ski way before they could get into the air.

'You are cleared for take-off. See you later.' With a cheery wave the air traffic controller elf gave the go ahead. Mrs Claus released the brakes and with a burst of acceleration the Reindeer headed down the ski way. In seconds the vibrating sleigh grew calm, and Mrs Claus knew she was airborne. She pulled down her goggles (which were hidden in a special pocket in the brim of her hat) and was away.

'South zero point zero one degrees, estimated time of arrival midnight plus zero point zero, zero, zero one seconds.' The navigator elf was enjoying himself. He was a veteran of many journeys with Santa, and was delighted to be back in the air.

The first drop was to a research station in the Arctic. Mrs Claus knew that the box of gifts (some furry gloves, a set of handwarmers, a packet of special hot chocolate with a chocolate dipper) would be very welcome to the lonely scientists working there. They landed, and in a flash the presents were delivered. They were away again so quickly that not even Leaky had time to leave one of his own special little presents.

'Next stop, Attu. Heading south by south, south West, zero point eight degrees. Estimated time of arrival, midnight plus five point six two seconds.'

Attu is a special island in a chain off the coast of Alaska. Most of those islands would not receive their visits for almost twenty four hours, when the earth had completed a full circle. But Attu was just on the other side of the international date line; it was already Christmas Day there (but only just). Usually the island of Attu did not feature on Santa's visits because it had been uninhabited for many years. But recently an old man who used to work there had returned to live. His family were visiting for Christmas (and that is easier said than done) including seven year old Anaya.

Anaya was the perfect reason that Mrs Claus had taken up delivery of the 'Specials.' Her mini sledge was waiting to be delivered next. A sledge would be a real treat for her. The detour to Attu would have taken her husband nearly five seconds out of his way. Now, that might not seem a lot, but when you have many deliveries to make it can be the difference between success and Boxing Day.

Attu is cold and icy and full of mountains, but the smoke lifting from the small hut near the sea helped the navigator elf, and soon the delivery was done. The reindeer even got their first taste of carrot – Anaya was a very thoughtful girl.

And so the midnight hour continued. Mrs Claus delivered hundreds of gifts in that time. On little islands and ships and even a submarine (which was pretty tricky, still periscopes have their uses). All was going well.

Leaky enjoyed being over the sea – nobody noticed when he needed to go, as long as he aimed carefully. Astro was still not quite himself, but the other reindeer were working together as the great team they were.

3

A Very Unusual Destination

'A tricky one next, Mrs Claus,' said the Navigator Elf. 'It's a bit unusual. An old fashioned pirate ship in the Pacific Ocean. Nobody is quite sure what they are up to, and being pirates they won't be getting any gifts.'

'So why are we going there?' asked the pilot.

'Well, there's a child on board. A cabin boy called Wilf. He's a lovely lad, despite all the no-goods he lives with. Santa thought he deserved something,' came the reply.

Their destination was already in sight when the news came in. 'Engine trouble; port side three.' The chief Engineer Elf was calm. Mrs Claus' sleigh could fly on seven Reindeer, although it would slow them down. Port side three was Astro, who had seemed out of sorts since they took off.

'Status report,' she requested.

'Reindeer reports a tummy ache,' came the worrying reply.

A quick decision was needed. 'OK, we'll land, deliver the present and review the situation. Prepare for docking.'

Mrs Claus was a good captain.

They saw the Pirate Ship grow larger as they descended from their cruising height. It looked odd to eyes used to giant tankers and luxury yachts on the water. Three masts were tied with rigging, and sails billowed with the Pacific wind. Although it was night time, the Pirates were making headway. This could be tricky.

'We need to find a landing place where we are out of sight,' instructed Mrs Claus. But her worry soon went away. Yes, there was a look out on board, but he was slumped in the crows' nest at the top of the tallest mast. A jar of something lay uncorked beside him.

On deck, another man lay propped up by the ship's wheel. He was resting against some chests, probably filled with treasure. The wheel was tied and rocked the ship in a straight line. A bottle of lager tinkled and leaked among many empties littering the wheel house. As they came in, a slight wave made the bottle roll, and more lager leaked out.

But maybe, Mrs Claus thought, as they landed, these were better pirates than their reputation suggested. On the deck were a number of carrots, a bucket of water, labelled with the word 'Raindear' (Pirates are bad spellers). To her surprise there was a plate of gorgeous looking mince pies (spelled 'mine pise').

Wilf's present was delivered, left in a rough sack hanging hopefully on his cabin door. Inside another gift was already there. A piece of paper with the words: 'IOU one prezent,

Priate Dad.' Meanwhile, the engineer elf checked on Astro. The reindeer was sniffing excitedly at the carrots and enjoying a welcome drink from the bucket.

'I think I'll have a mince pie while we wait,' smiled Mrs Claus.

She picked up a beautiful, buttery, flaky mince pie and bit into its spicy middle.

** BOOM!! **

The explosion shook her. She threw the pie into the air, and saw its fruity filling fall onto her white scarf. It's dappled spots making her scarf look like the coat of a dalmatian.

The label had not been wrong. They *were* 'mine' pies! And the reason for them being left soon became clear. From below decks swarmed a group of men with dark beards, patches over their eyes, even a wooden leg or two. The two drunk men had only been pretending. They stood and cheered.

'It worked!' they screamed.

'What's going on?' asked Mrs Claus, determined to stay calm and in charge.

4

Kidnapped

A tall and particularly mean looking man stepped forward. He carried an old fashioned pistol, and a cutlass sat in the belt of his trousers. A plastic penguin sat on his shoulders.

'Oooh aah,' he said, with a sideways movement of his head. 'You be kidnapped. Ha ha. I be got your sleigh and all your presents, little Miss Christmas.'

'It's Mrs Claus to you,' said Mrs C in her best teacher's voice. 'And take that penguin off your shoulder. It looks ridiculous.'

'What be you meaning, woman?' the pirate asked, 'I be 'Cap'n Crow and this be me 'awk. You be walkin' the plank into the ol' briny if you don't watch your step.'

'It's a plastic penguin,' she told him.

'Well you try t'find 'awks out 'ere,' Captain Crow looked like he'd been told off. 'Anyways, we's gonna take your treasure. It'll be like Christmas, hee hee.' He raised his arms and fired the pistol in the air. The pirates cheered, and the man in the crow's nest let out a squawk and tumbled to the deck.

'You need to be careful where you're pointing your pistol,' admonished Mrs Claus.

''E be food for the sharks now,' said the wicked captain, rolling the poor pirate over the side. 'Right men, empty that sleigh!'

'You'll never catch us in this old cutter. Reindeer, prepare to…'

Mrs Claus stopped in her tracks as engineer Elf tapped her on the shoulder. She turned to look and saw seven sleeping reindeer. Astro was still standing, but looking very uncomfortable. 'The carrots were covered in sleeping powder,' explained the engineer. 'They all had some except Astro, whose tummy hurt too much. We're stuck!'

Mrs Claus thought that she might have been better off at home in the North Pole, but only for a second. She was a woman of action. A bunch of pirates was nothing to be scared of.

She was just thinking this when a smiling face appeared from below decks. A couple of arms rose in the air, and the face stretched into a yawn. Then, halfway through, the face stopped, unsure which emotion to express first.

At first, Wilf's expressed happiness, it was Christmas after all. Then horror at the site of the pirates ready for battle. Next it showed astonishment, as he saw a lady dressed all in red with white trim, a couple of small elves dressed in green by her side. Then it was the turn of wonder as the face took in the gleaming sleigh, with all it's lights blinking. Finally, it was sadness as the sleeping reindeer came into view.

'What's going on?' the face had the voice of a boy.

'You get back down below decks, cabin boy,' the Captain spoke, and his penguin wobbled as he turned to face the boy.

'Dad. What have you been up to?'

'Avast ye child, get thee abaft and below.'

'Dad...' the boy sounded rather disapproving.

'These landlubbers have bought the booty,' the boy's father went on. His eyes began to move shiftily from side to side. 'and you do as you are told or I'll be tickling you on the dungbie; thou'll be shark bait before thee can utter "Shiver me timbers" and "Yo ho ho!"'

Mrs Claus was looking in amazement at this exchange. Despite all the threats the boy seemed completely unfazed.

'Dad, you've been up to something. I always know because you start talking in that silly pirate language. Now, be nice to the lady, offer her a cup of tea so we can sort out whatever it is that you've done.'

'Come thee hither boy,' the pirate roared, but the boy put his hands firmly on his hips and stood where he was. It was all rather discouraging to the pirate. He walked over to the boy, bent down and whispered in his ear. 'Wilf, I've got my reputation with these cut throats to keep up.'

He pointed at the assembled pirates, many of whom were now grinning, and some were beginning to laugh. 'Close thee mouths, scallywags, or thy'll be walking the plank by dawn.' The Captain's shout stopped the laughter, but the pirates were still smiling with their eyes.

The Captain once more bent down to Wilf. 'Lookee here, Wilf,' he persuaded, 'that old sleigh is weighed down with treasure. We didn't ask the old lady to land here, she's the one who's trespassing. I think that makes those wrapped up presents mine…ours.'

Wilf was not going to be easily convinced by the Captain's smooth words. 'It's no surprise she's here, is it. Look what you've done to her reindeer. It's Christmas dad. Goodwill to everybody.'

'Oh they'll be awake in moment. Just a little sleeping powder on a carrot.'

In fact, as Captain Crow was speaking, the reindeer were beginning to wake up.

'Quick lads, get the presents before they escape!'

5

The Stolen Presents

Captain Crow led the way, rushing to the sleigh. With much pulling and tearing, he started to remove the gifts that were meant for deserving children and adults. The pirates followed suit. Even Wilf's cries of 'No, leave them' made no difference.

Soon the deck was covered with beautifully wrapped parcels. There was no more room, but the sleigh was still full.

'Drop the anchor, we need to think about this,' said Captain Crow. He sat on a pile of boxes, which began to flatten under his weight. Then, with a tinkle of broken glass, he fell to the deck.

'There goes Mrs Smith's crystal vase. She's been hoping for that for five years,' said Mrs Claus with annoyance.

'Aye, mebbee, but what about my bum,' he said, rubbing hard.

'You deserve everything you get!' Mrs Claus was offering no sympathy.

Near the wheel the coxswain found the whole incident rather funny.

As the moonlight peeped out from behind the clouds, everyone could suddenly see something awful. Awfully funny, that is. The Captain's bare bottom was peeping through the hole in his breeches, made by the broken glass.

'See your bum,' he laughed 'we all can, you've torn your breeches.'

Captain Crow felt behind him and pulled at the tatters of his trousers.

'Why you rapscallion…it's in the briny for you!' he rushed towards the Coxswain, who immediately stopped laughing. The ocean looked cold, and dark.

But Captain Crow had overlooked something. Leaky had enjoyed a long sleep, and had been standing with his legs crossed for some time now. He could hold on no longer. As the wicked pirate raced over the deck, the dry wood suddenly turned wet…and very slippery.

Captain Crow's legs shot out in front of him. His arms waved for a second or two, then with a loud 'thump' he hit the deck. He sat still for a moment, then slowly toppled backwards until he lay directly under Leaky.

'Not the best place to sit!' laughed Mrs Claus. He was not finished yet, and the Pirate got his morning shower earlier than was usual.

All the Pirates laughed. Wilf doubled over, clutching his sides as he watched the warm water trickled down his father's face. Even Mrs Claus smiled.

Astro's tummy started to gurgle and rumble loudly. "I told him, he shouldn't have eaten all the apples", said Mrs Claus

'Get those presents opened,' ordered Captain Crow angrily. He did not like to be made to look foolish. He grabbed one and got ready to tear off the paper; then he saw the label. 'To Grandad, lots of love, Sasha' it said. 'I hope that this takes your mind off gran for a couple of minutes. Miss you lots.' She had written the message and sent it for Santa to stick on her present.

Sasha, whoever she was, had drawn a heart with two old people holding hands on the label. The pirate chief paused for a moment, thinking back to his own grandad. 'Well, maybe we'll leave this one,' he said, gently putting the present back into the sleigh.

But it was as though this show of kindness had shocked the pirate, and he roared angrily: 'Get opening, it's our lucky day. Christmas, hah, Christmas for us!' The pirates moved uncertainly towards the presents. Wilf stepped forward to stop them as best as he could. Then he caught Mrs Claus' eyes, and they said to him to bide his time.

She gave the smallest smile, and he nodded, waiting to see what would happen next.

The first present opened was by Midshipman Mark, a particularly unpleasant pirate. 'Ha, we're not going to make a fortune on that!' he said, looking at the beautifully detailed model penguin in his hand. 'Childish tat!' and with a swing of the arms, he threw the toy over board, where it hit the waves and sank slowly to the bottom of the ocean.

'Where it belongs. Well done Midshipman Mark,' roared Captain Crow, opening his own first stolen gift.

'Young Sasha will be sad. There'll be no present for her from her granddad this year. Still, she won't mind, she'll think he's too sad to remember. Never mind, there's plenty of walruses where she lives, not many penguins, though.' Mrs Claus spoke quietly.

'Well, maybe you were a little hasty, Midshipman…or, deckhand as you now are!'

Ex-midshipman Mark thought about arguing, but something in his Captain's eyes told him not to.

Captain Crow put down the present he was about to open, and looked at his crew and the goodies they were starting to reveal.

First Mate Frank held up a lovely set of dolls, all dressed in uniforms of nurses and doctors. 'We can sell this when we dock!' grinned Frank.

'Yes,' said Mrs Claus, 'that's a good idea. Although, you won't get near the value of it.'

'We'll do well enough!' boasted the First Mate.

'Perhaps you will,' came the reply. 'It was for Millie, whose mummy is a doctor deep in the jungle. She has to work on Christmas day, so she thought that Millie could pretend to be a doctor as well, then she might not miss her mummy too much.'

'Perhaps you should wrap that one up again,' ordered Captain Crow, at half volume (which was still pretty loud).

Next Quincy the Quartermaster opened a plastic cutlass,

bejewelled with coloured stones. 'Hah, I'll keep this myself,' he roared, swishing it around his head and threatening to whack a nearby shipmate.

'You do that,' advised Mrs Claus. 'It was for Brian. His mummy and daddy haven't got much money but they know that he loves pirates. They saved up for weeks to buy him that. There's a pirate's uniform somewhere in the pile of presents around your feet. It won't fit you, but why don't you take that as well. Brian knows his mummy and daddy haven't got much money, so he won't be expecting anything. They live in a little shed, you know, halfway up a mountain. There's no work for Daddy when it snows.'

Quincy stopped waving the sword around. He stuck it in his waistband.

Shaun the Shipmate was next. 'Ah, a silver picture frame. This'll be worth a few bottles of grog. I'll just take out this rubbish picture.' He started to open the frame, to remove the picture of a dog smiling up at the camera that had captured its image.

'Ah, Georgie. He's lovely, isn't he?' explained Mrs Claus. 'That picture was meant for Jack; he had to move to a small island because of his daddy's job. Georgie's quite old, and he wouldn't have managed that journey. The photo was sent by Georgie's new owner, just to show that he was getting on well.'

Wilf noticed that the deck had gone quiet. Those pirates with presents in their hand had stopped unwrapping. There were thoughtful expressions on their faces.

'Come on men, let's get this treasure opened.' Captain Crow tried to get his men going again, and seized a present himself, tearing off the wrapping. Inside was a new iPad. 'Jackpot!' Captain Crow waved it in the air. He was expecting cheers from his men, but there was just the occasional grunt. Most looked away.

'And don't give me some soppy story about this.'

'I won't,' said Mrs Claus. 'It's for Jill. She's in hospital. Her mummy is looking after her sisters, because they live on an island without a hospital on it. Her mum thought that Jill could see them on Christmas Day, but a phone call will be good enough. It's a shame though, but if you want it more…

Captain Crow had seen enough. Beneath that cross body beat a kindly heart, although he tried to keep it a secret. 'Ok, Ok, stop. Men, put the presents back – wrap up the ones you've opened – yes Quartermaster, even the cutlass and let this lady get back to delivering presents,' he said.

They did so, but still Mrs Claus did not get on board her sleigh. 'Look to the horizon,' she said. And there, with an orange glow, the sun was rising.

6

Christmas is Cancelled

'We can move West and catch up with night again,' she said, 'but with Astro not firing properly, we'll never get all the presents delivered in time.'

She sat very still, looking down at her feet. A tear slid down her face, as she pictured the children who would wake up to find an empty stocking. The mood fell.

The pirates, elves and Mrs Claus scratched their heads. The reindeers even scratched their chins which, trust me, is not easy for a reindeer.

'There's one chance,' the Engineer Elf spoke up. Every pirate eye looked hopefully at the Elf. 'It means you pirates have to help.' All the eyes moved to look at Captain Crow.

Captain Crow had had enough of being a pirate for one day. For once, he had no doubts about what he should do. 'Mrs Claus' he said. 'We got you into this mess, we ought to help you out of it.'

'Oh dad!' Wilf hugged his father, who looked a bit embarrassed, but smiled anyway.

'If we attach the pirate ship to the sleigh, when we get in the air, the wind will fill the sails and be like a second engine. We'll get a burst of speed, and catch up the lost time.'

'Go for it!' screamed the Pirates together. Within seconds Mrs Claus was on board, the sleigh was roped to the ship and they were off…nowhere. The reindeer's strained and pulled and tugged, even Astro did his best but it was no good. The ship hardly moved.

'The Anchor!' Captain Crow shouted the answer. His crew ran to release it; but it would not move. It was stuck.

'Keep trying!' encouraged Mrs Claus to anybody who would listen. The Reindeer strained, the crew pulled at the anchor, the Elves used their brains. But for poor Astro it was too much. He plonked himself down and refused to move.

'Reindeer down,' reported the engineer Elf. 'We'll never get free with just seven. It looks like the children living far away from anybody else, or in hospital or on a small island will just have to manage. They'll understand. Good children always do.'

'What is wrong with the reindeer?' asked Captain Crow.

'Fuel blockage,' explained engineer Elf. 'Astro ate too many apples and they've given him a bad tummy ache. He's all clogged up inside. It'll clear in time, but it could take hours. And we don't have hours.'

They stood shaking their heads. Even Mrs Claus had run out of ideas. It was Wilf who came up with *THE IDEA*. 'Dad,' he said. 'You sometimes get a blocked up tummy. You know, after you've drunk too many bottles of rum and eaten a bit bag of fish and chips?'

'What's that got to do with the price of gold?' asked Captain Crow, annoyed at the interruption.

'Well, you take some of your special powder, then you go into the toilet. Then everything's ok. Apart from the toilet.'

'You know, you're right Wilf. Tummy medicine should do the trick. Quartermaster, bring up the tummy medicine.

7

Astro Saves The Day

Knowing quite how much to put into a reindeer was hard to judge. The powder was not to be used by children, but a reindeer is bigger than that, so they hoped it would be ok. 'Start with four tablespoons in a bucket of water,' instructed Shaggy, the Ship's doctor.

He wasn't a very good doctor, and so the pirates decided to double the dose. After all, a reindeer is quite big. Astro looked rather worried, but took his medicine. 'Walk him around a bit, I find it helps me if I move about,' said Captain Crow.

They were at the poop deck, at the back of the ship, when it happened. The poop deck was the perfect place. Astro stopped and looked curious. Then he looked worried, then scared and then relieved. It was what happened between being scared and being relieved that was important.

Out of Astro's rear end roared a wind like a hurricane. It burst into the sails, filling them. The ship lurched, then with a snap the chain holding the anchor split, and crashed into the water. The ship had broken free.

'Take Off!' roared Mrs Claus. With the reindeer galloping across the night sky, the sleigh and the ship moved like lightning.

Then, for a micro second, the sails began to lose their energy. Everyone held their breath. Just at that moment the real wind caught the sails and they burst forwards again. As they surged forward, there was a loud cheer from the pirates.

Astro rushed to take his place in the engine room, adding even more speed to the sleigh.

'Captain Crow, you saved the day!' shouted Mrs Claus. There was a cheer, but as everybody on board sought to congratulate the good pirate, it died in their throat. Captain Crow was nowhere to be seen. Had he been blown overboard by Astro's windy release?

At the back of the ship stood a brown statue; it had not been there before. As all eyes were staring at the statue, the statue raised one arm. Two spots of white popped open where its eyes should be. Captain Crow had taken the full force of Astro's explosion. It was not a pretty sight. Nor was it a pretty smell.

The crew cowered, even Wilf looked concerned. He stepped a few paces closer to the statue.

'Dad?' he whispered.

Then a white line cut across the head of the statue, teeth glowed and two arms wiped hard, revealing a smiling, shining (but still rather pooh-brown) face. 'Captain Crow and his Crew

TO THE RESCUE!' He grabbed a cloth, cleaned his Penguin and then himself. 'Let's get going, there's presents to be delivered!' he screamed.

Pirates and elves worked hard that night. They travelled at the speed of light, they found boats in the ocean, huts in mountains, lonely hospitals and solitary boarding schools. And soon there was only one more house to visit.

It was a small community on a tiny island, the houses with metal walls. Scientific equipment was littered around. In the darkness it was just about possible to make out a sign. It read 'Aleutian Islands Walrus Preservation Research'.

A nightlight shone through one window, where a small girl could be seen sleeping. A stocking was hanging from the end of her bed. Some home made snowflakes hung from her ceiling, and there were plenty of real ones outside.

'Sasha's Room' was spelt out in coloured letters on the other side of her open bedroom door. On a shelf stood a collection of model penguins, and in the centre was a large gap.

'Ah well, nothing for Sasha any more. Hers ended up in the ocean I seem to remember,' said Mrs Claus, lifting presents labelled with the names of her parents. 'But she'll enjoy watching her mummy and daddy open their gifts, and at least they are together for Christmas. Sometimes families are separated when parents are working a long way from home.'

Mrs Claus sighed, she didn't like to see any child disappointed.

'Wait a minute,' she heard Captain Crow call. He crept up to the sack, and inside placed a large gift, wrapped in ship's sacking. Mrs Claus looked, and noticed that his penguin was gone from his shoulder.

Captain Crow smiled.

With the last present delivered, it was time to say their goodbyes.

There was much back slapping between the pirates and the elves. Meanwhile, Mrs Claus gave young Wilf a big hug and whispered 'See you again, next Christmas!' before jumping on to the sleigh and heading off.

The ship headed south, to warmer waters, and Mrs Claus set off north for a special dinner with Santa Claus and the elves, to be followed by a good long rest.

8

Back at the North Pole

Back at the North Pole, Santa and Mrs Claus were enjoying a nice cup of coffee. They were full of lovely food, and warm in the thought that once again there were children all around the world waking up to gifts of love.

'Record time…thanks to you,' laughed Santa. 'We positively whooshed across the oceans not having to keep stopping for a ship or an almost uninhabited island.'

He paused for a second and took another sip of his coffee.

'We were so far ahead, we had a little rest in Barbados and watched the waves coming in under the stars. We were a whole second ahead of schedule. The reindeer didn't know what was happening.'

He smiled at the thought, yawned and all was quiet for a moment. Soon, the sound of snoring reached Mrs Claus' ears and she glanced at her husband and saw his coffee cup perched precariously on his tummy. She got it, took it carefully, and put it on the table.

Mrs Claus looked at her sleeping husband, his bulging tummy rising and falling steadily, and she smiled.

She couldn't wait to see what adventures she'd have next year, and neither could Leena, Inara, Anneli, Ansa, Thomas, Tapio, Astro or …. Leaky.

9

A Present for Captain Crow

A few hours later, the ship was far enough south for Captain Crow to be sure they wouldn't bump into an iceberg. He decided to get some rest. He was still a little smelly, and fancied a bath. It would be his Christmas present to himself.

He had his soak (in Pirate Bubble Bath, of course) then headed to his room for a good snooze. There, on his pillow, sat a small box, with a tiny red bow and shiny red paper covering it.

A little label was pushed under the ribbon. It just said: 'Thanks, Mrs C.'

Captain Crow felt tears coming into his eyes, he hadn't received a present since his Grandad had died when he was just a little boy. They were tears of remembering, of happiness and of knowing he had done a good deed. He decided to wait to open the gift. He knew he'd enjoy it more when he was wider awake.

So it was many hours later that he took the box and carefully unwrapped it. Inside was a small box of raisins. He loved raisins; he would really enjoy them.

Captain Crow took the raisins up on deck. He'd share them with Wilf, he decided. Next year, he would make sure the boy got a real Christmas Present instead of an IOU. But for now, they could share the raisins together.

He opened the box and shook some into his son's hand. He popped one into his own mouth and chewed with pleasure. His second raisin was held up, ready to follow the first, when Wilf pointed – his jaw dropping open.

'Polite pirates don't eat with their mouths open...' Captain Crow started to say, then he saw why the boy was pointing. An object was getting closer. It was blue and red and yellow and orange and all colours of the rainbow.

Soon they could see it was a bird, and then, with a whoosh of wings and a squawk the raisin was snatched from Captain Crow's hand.

He felt a thump on his shoulder and looked...straight into the face of a *real, live parrot*.

'Hello Dad, 'ello Dad, 'ello dad,' it squawked. 'Nice raisin.'

THE END

Mrs Claus and the Christmas Stowaway

MRS CLAUS HELPS SANTA DELIVER
THE PRESENTS DESPITE SABOTAGE
AT THE NORTH POLE : A
CHILDREN'S CHRISTMAS STORY FOR
AGES 4-8

1

A Tournament at the North Pole

Lights flashed as dozens of elf cameras clicked, trying to capture Mrs Claus's greatest snowboarding run yet this season.

She really was on a roll. Her adventures delivering Christmas gifts, had really helped her confidence.

There'd been weeks of intense training for the event. This year Mrs Claus felt better prepared than ever before.

She'd nearly completed the course, it had all gone perfectly. Now, she was getting ready for something really special. She was going to finish her run with a secret move she had been working on. She'd been practising it for weeks.

Mrs Claus's silver all-in-one suit glittered, and her goggles twinkled, as the cameras flashed.

As she started the descent of the final run, Mrs Claus felt such elation. As crisp air stung her face, she sped down the last slope and onto the ramp.

Everything was going just as she'd practiced it, until her keen eye noticed something, just a moment too late. She saw that the ramp had moved, just ever so slightly.

Oh no! She saw it too late and took the ramp too slowly! As she launched into her triple-twist mega-jump move, she knew it was all going wrong. She spun in the air for a moment, then met with the ground with a sickening sound ... CRUNCH! AHHHHAAAGH!

Instead of the smooth landing she'd been practicing for months, Mrs Claus had crash landed!

As she hit the ground, she felt her foot bending one way and her leg bending another. A sharp pain shot up her leg. 'Ouch! That hurt!'

Santa Claus had been watching on the sidelines. At the sight of her crashing, he rushed over. 'Are you alright, my love?' He went pale, frowning as he saw how much pain she was in (it looked rather strange for a man who usually had a jolly face and rosy cheeks).

'No, I'm afraid not!' cried Mrs Claus. 'Someone moved the ramp! What on earth happened? Has someone sabotaged the tournament? Perhaps someone didn't want me to win this year.'

'Shhh, it's going to be alright,' whispered Santa. 'If someone did sabotage the run, we'll find out who it is. Right now, we must get you to the medic elves. We need to see what damage you've done to yourself, my love.'

Santa wasn't sure that the ramp looked any different. He wondered if Mrs Claus had been a little over-ambitious with her final move. However, he had been married for long enough to know that now was not the time to discuss the matter with his injured wife!

'I'm afraid it looks like you've broken your ankle,' said the chief medic elf. 'We're going to have to put it in plaster, so it can heal. No more snowboarding for you. You need to rest your leg and take it easy for a few weeks.'

'Oh, my dear," said Mrs Claus, blinking away tears. "There's only three weeks to go until we deliver the presents on Christmas Eve. Whatever shall we do?"

Tears ran down Mrs Claus's face, as she realised that she may not be able to help Santa deliver the presents this year.

'Don't worry, my dear, I can manage,' said Santa. He attempted his usual chortle, but it sounded strained. The look in his eye told Mrs Claus what she already knew, he really *did* need her help.

2

Back at the North Pole

Santa and Mrs Claus sat in their favourite arm chairs by the fire in their cosy home in the North Pole.

Snow was steadily falling outside and settling on the roof and window sills of the cabin. The sounds of the elves working next door was such a happy sound. Their magnificent decorated Christmas tree looked like a scene straight out of a Christmas card.

But things were different this Christmas.

When Mrs Claus had broken her ankle at the snowboarding competition, the medics elves had put a big plaster on her foot. She'd been hobbling around for weeks now. She knew that there was no way she'd be able to climb down the chimneys to deliver the children's presents this year.

Santa had begun to rely on her to help him with his increasing work load on Christmas Eve. She was particularly helpful when it came to delivering presents to some of the remotest locations.

With quite so many children all around the world, it was almost impossible for it to be a job for just *one* man any more. Even if that man was Santa Claus himself!

Without Mrs Claus, Santa was struggling to find a way he'd be able to get presents delivered to everyone around the world, before the sun came up on Christmas Day.

'Oh I'm as cross as a hairy baboon!' Santa exclaimed.

'Baboons aren't cross dear,' said Mrs Claus soothingly, 'not even hairy ones.'

'We still haven't found out who moved the ramp. I just know it was sabotage!' proclaimed Santa.

'I know you're frustrated, my love, but no one saw anyone move the ramp at the competition. I just hope that we find them, before they do any more harm,' said Mrs Claus.

'I'm quite sure that you would have made that jump, my dear,' replied Santa.

When all their investigations had come up dry, Mrs Claus had begun to doubt herself. 'I know you think that I'm going nuttier than squirrel poo. I'd practiced that move for months and perfected it. I would have aced it too, if someone hadn't moved the ramp,' said Mrs Claus. 'I just wish I was going to helping out this year.'

'Now, I don't want you to worry about the deliveries, my dear. With a little help from the reindeer, I'm sure I'll be able to make them all this year.'

3

The Day before Christmas Eve

It was the day before Christmas Eve. Mrs Claus called it Christmas Eve, Eve. She rather liked the sound of it.

Santa was busy in his workshop, attending to a few last minute hiccups, whilst the elves were loading the sleigh.

There was a knock on the door, and Mrs Claus opened the door to Zippy, her chief engineer.

'Mrs Claus, I've made you an early Christmas present,' she squeaked excitedly. She'd been working on this for days and was impatient to show her what she'd made.

'Thank you, Zippy. Please put it under the tree with the other presents,' said Mrs Claus, showing the elf inside.

Her voice was low and sad. It had been a tough couple of weeks, watching all the preparations being made and knowing she'd be staying home this year.

After Santa gave her a sleigh of her own, she'd been so excited, all year, to take another trip around the world. And it wasn't just her who was feeling disappointed, Leena, Inara, Anneli and Ansa, Astro, Leaky, Thomas and Tapio, the reindeer, were all hanging their heads and feeling rather envious of Rudolf and the other reindeers.

'Oh no, Mrs Claus! You need to open it *right now!*' Zippy could barely contain herself.

Mrs Claus looked at the gift Zippy was holding out to her. The large box was wrapped in bright red wrapping paper, with a glittering, golden bow on the top. Bursting with curiosity, Mrs Claus started tearing the paper that sealed the box.

As she looked inside, her curiosity turned to shock, then to bemused bewilderment. 'Zippy... what is it?' asked Mrs Claus, rather embarrassed that she didn't know already.

'Some of the engineering elves put our heads together and designed this for you. We saw how sad you were when you thought you couldn't help Santa this year and decided to do something about it.'

'It's a jet pack. Instead of climbing down the chimneys, you can hover up from the sleigh and then hover down them. It's just like flying. If you want to help Santa deliver the presents this year, then you can,' said Zippy happily.

Looking up, she saw an enormous smile lighting up Mrs Claus's face.

'Try it on for size,' she suggested.

Mrs Claus pulled on the black jet pack. It was as light as a feather and streamlined for speed. On the black straps were two metal rods covered with buttons. She pulled down the rods and pressed one of the buttons.

Instantly, she felt herself being lifted up. When she looked down, she could see she was hovering a couple of inches above the ground.

'Oh my goodness, this is really something. It actually works!' she gasped.

She pressed another button, and begun moving this way and that across the room. She was hovering several centimetres above the floor, much to the concern of her puzzled-looking cat.

Mrs Claus was so excited, she swung open the front door and ran outside.

She was busy experimenting with all the buttons, working out how everything worked and enjoying her new 'toy'.

She hovered straight past Santa's workshop.

WHOOOSH!!

When he saw his wife speeding past his workshop on what looked like a jet pack, poor Santa spilled hot chocolate all down his front.

He rubbed his eyes, thinking he'd accidentally put some of Dizzy's special brandy in his chocolate (it was pretty strong stuff, usually reserved for the post-delivery Christmas party)

'I'm going to deliver the presents after all!' Mrs Claus called out to him, whilst she hovered in circles outside the workshop.

'The elves made this, so I can still give the presents to the children!'

'I wonder what happens if I press this …,' thought Mrs Claus, as she pressed a few more buttons. She rose higher, swooped and dived. She was doing a loop the loop, high in the air.

"Whooooppeeeeee!' she cried out.

As she came out of the loop, her stomach did a little flip. 'Hmmm,' she thought to herself, 'I better not do that again when I've got a tummy full of mince pieces, who knows what might happen?'

Once Mrs Claus had landed safely, she was beaming from ear to ear. After all the sadness and worry of the last few weeks, she could hardly believe what was happening.

'I don't know what to say,' said Mrs Claus. 'I'm simply amazed by the ingenuity of your elf engineering team, Zippy! Thank you.'

'Sorry your jet pack isn't red, to match the sleigh. We thought stealth would be better than style this year. We've even got you combat jacket and trousers, to keep you warm and keep you stealthy. There are so many children to deliver presents to this year, you don't want to attract any unwanted attention.'

'Oh my goodness me!' Mrs Claus cried. 'We have so much to do and so little time. How are we ever going to be ready in time for take-off tomorrow evening? Round up the troops! Brush down the reindeer! Hose down the sleigh!'

'Don't worry, it's all in hand, Mrs Claus,' said the elf. 'When we realised our invention was going to work, we put all the usual preparations in place.'

'Your sleigh is polished and gleaming. The reindeer are ready. Everything's set for tomorrow night. All you need to do is get a good night's sleep. So, goodnight and Merry Christmas, Mrs Claus!'

And off she went, that marvellous little elf, to make sure that everything was ready for Mrs Claus.

4

The Girl, the Woods and the Treehouse

Thousands of miles away from the North Pole, stood a wooden cabin, deep in the forest. A sparkling Christmas tree stood outside, with more fairy lights than the Eiffel Tower.

Inside the cabin, a young girl with long, curly hair was getting ready for bed. She had been waiting so long for this special night. She and her daddy had been building a treehouse in a nearby tree. They started in spring, when the first leaves were appearing on the trees and finished two days before Christmas Eve, just in time for the celebrations.

They had to think long and hard about which of the nearby trees in the forest would be just right to build their treehouse in. It had to have low sprawling branches to support the structure, yet not be too high off the ground.

Finally, they found the perfect tree, right at the edge of the woodland clearing. Juliet and her dad had such fun together, using every single tool in daddy's toolbox for their project.

They'd created the most amazing, secret hideaway that any girl could wish for.

A wooden ladder led up to the treehouse itself. There was a large window, that looked down over Juliet's home. It was a cozy cabin, with it's own front door. There was a hatch in the roof that lifted up, so that Juliet could look straight up at the stars at nighttime.

Her dad had made two little stools and a table for Juliet to sit at. She had a stack of her favorite books, so that she could lie here and disappear into the magical world of their fabulous stories.

Having her own Christmas hideaway really was the best Christmas gift she could have wished for.

Her parents had agreed that she could sleep in the treehouse for the first time on Christmas Eve. She was *so* excited. She'd dreamt of seeing Santa every Christmas Eve, but always seemed to miss the magic moment. She was desperate to spot Santa, and longed for the moment when she'd see his jolly red hat disappearing down her chimney.

Her parents thought that she would fall asleep, long before Santa came to call. The girl was determined to prove them wrong, and felt sure that this year was the year when she'd catch her first glimpse of Santa, though the windows of the treehouse.

It was time for her to go to bed, in her very own treehouse. She was so excited, she was sure she wouldn't be able to sleep a wink. Mum and dad walked across the woodland clearing with her, to help her carry the bedding to the treehouse.

'Goodnight mum, goodnight dad. I'll see you in the morning!'

She climbed the ladder, up to the treehouse. And just like that, her Christmas Eve adventure had begun.

She unpacked her duvet, her sleeping bag, her hot water bottle (filled and toasty warm, thanks to her mummy), her fluffy Christmas socks (the ones with the bobble on the toes) and her reindeer-print all-in-one pyjamas.

She was desperate to try and stay awake in the treehouse until Santa arrived. She laid the small table carefully with the milk and mince pies, not forgetting the cream and a napkin.

She planned to be cozy and warm. She hoped to spot Santa and invite him into the treehouse for glass of milk and a mince pie, while the reindeer ate the pile of freshly dug carrots she'd left at the bottom of the ladder.

Next, she wriggled down deep into her sleeping bag and tucked the duvet around her body. She was willing herself not to fall asleep, keeping a hand on her torch, ready to catch a glimpse of the man in red.

The girls name was Juliet.

5

The Figure In The Black Hat

That same Christmas Eve Eve, not far from Mrs Claus's cozy house, sat someone who wasn't feeling at all Christmassy.

In a dark room, in a dark house, a figure in a dark coat and a black hat was sitting by a roaring fire, thinking dark thoughts.

This was the only house in the North Pole that wasn't ablaze with lights, both inside and out. There were no Christmas lights, no Christmas tree and no stocking hung by the fireplace.

The dark figure paced up and down in front of the fire.

'Santa used to only need me to do the deliveries. And now *she* comes in and has her own sleigh and her own reindeer team. Its not fair, if anyone should have their own sleigh and reindeer team, it should be me,' thought the figure in the black hat.

'How many deliveries have I helped Santa complete? Hundreds? Probably thousands! Its not fair. It should be me.'

'But I'm going to show her. I'll show all of them. They shouldn't have let her have her own sleigh and reindeer. After that whole thing with the pirates last Christmas, that was a disgrace to present-delivering.'

'Mrs Claus deserved what she got, snowboarding at *her* age. Even if I hadn't moved the ramp, she'd have probably broken something anyway.'

'I'll show them, I'll show all of them. They'll come crawling back and beg me to take over the special deliveries. Then, I'll get *my* sleigh and *my* reindeer. Yes, they'll see.'

Pulling on a coat, the figure stomped out into the snow.

6

Something Unexpected
Happens

It was Christmas Eve and the countdown had begun.

T minus 5, 4, 3, 2, 1 ….

TAKE OFF!

The two sleighs sped down the launch ramp, and up into the night sky.

'I'll meet you back her in the shake of a reindeer's antlers!' shouted Santa, as he headed off to his first stop, in the South Pacific.

'Looking forward to the party!' replied Mrs Claus. She was also looking forward to this year's holiday in Barbados, and had been itching to go back since their visit a few years ago.

'Hey, Zippy, is it me or does the sleigh feel a bit…well, off balance this year?' said Mrs Claus.

'Hmmm, I don't think so. Well, it shouldn't be,' replied Zippy.

'I carried out all the pre-flight checks myself. After that incident with the ramp, I've looked over every single inch of this sleigh twice, just to make sure.'

'I'm probably just being over cautious since I hurt my ankle. Let's have a look and see who's first on our list this year.'

She paused and read from her list. 'It seems we're off to a cabin in the woods, to see a girl called Juliet,' said Mrs Claus.

The cabin wasn't too hard to find, it was in a small clearing, at the end of a dirt track.

'What a beautiful home. It looks a little like mine back in the North Pole', said Mrs Claus approvingly.

Juliet had enjoyed helping her dad to build the treehouse so much that she'd written a letter to Santa asking him for her own set of tools this Christmas.

There were no street lights. The moon and stars were out in all their splendour, lighting the way for Mrs Claus and the reindeer. They parked up, halfway between the house and the treehouse.

Mrs Claus was busy adjusting and fiddling with the jet pack. She was too busy to notice a wide-eyed Juliet, looking at her from her treehouse.

Mrs Claus powered up the jet pack and glided smoothly over the forest floor. She unbolted the door and went inside the little house.

No magic key was needed for this house. Juliet's family didn't need a lock on their door, few people even knew there was a house hidden away here. The door was just there to keep out wandering woodland wildlife.

Juliet was staring in surprise and disbelief at the scene before her. A woman was gliding through the air in front of her and opening her front door. She sat frozen to the spot, looking out of the treehouse window at the sleigh and reindeer below.

Inside the house, if it wasn't for the Christmas tree and the glow from the fire inside, Mrs Claus wouldn't have been able to see where she was going at all. In the winter, the family kept the log fire burning all night, so they'd stay warm and snug all through the night.

Juliet stared in disbelief. 'That wasn't Santa! Who is this imposter?' she asked herself.

She was in shock. She had been waiting excitedly for Santa, and here was someone who was obviously *not* Santa, breaking into her house.

'What's happened to Santa? Is he OK? Has he been kidnapped?' thought Juliet.

Juliet was worried. She knew she had to go and check that he was alright, and not tied up somewhere with no one to help him.

So, Juliet unpeeled all the layers that she had been sleeping in, switched off her torch, and climbed silently down the ladder. She watched for a moment, as the reindeer tucked into the carrots, that she'd left out.

The reindeer were still waiting for Mrs Claus and feeling rather chilly in the winter air.

'I'm cold, let's go,' moaned Astro.

'I've got a cold!' said Leena with a shake. 'My antlers are shivering.' (Actually, what she said was 'I've dot a dold, mige Addlers ur shiddering' but nobody would understand that.)

'I need to go to the bathroom first,' said Leakey, crossing his hooves.

And it was while Leakey was standing behind a tree, making a tinkly sound, that Juliet made her move.

She crept slowly towards the sleigh, while Mrs Claus was inside, delivering the presents. She ducked around the back of the sleigh and jumped on board.

Sitting on the front seat she was an elf, wearing a smart green woollen dress. Fortunately for Juliet, just at that moment, the elf was looking toward the cabin, waiting for Mrs Claus to reappear.

She was on board the sleigh! Juliet breathed a sigh or relief.

7

A Stowaway on the Sleigh

Juliet pulled some sacks over her head, trying to find somewhere to sit while she figured out her next move.

Juliet settled down amongst the mountain of presents. It took a moment to take in her surroundings. There were presents everywhere!

Round ones and bumpy ones. Long thin presents and short fat presents. All of them were wrapped in beautiful paper and looked so, well, Christmassy. One of the presents had jolly sharp, pointy edges and was sticking right into her bottom. 'Ouch!' That wasn't very comfortable. She moved and sat on something soft and squishy.

'Owww!' Something screamed quietly in the darkness.

'Who's there?' Juliet whispered, a little scared of what the answer might be.

'Who are YOU?' a voice whispered in reply.

A shadowy figure wearing a dark coat and a black hat appeared.

'Who are you?' Juliet retorted. This was too much, first a fake Santa *and* now another stowaway on the sleigh?

'My name is Zappy, and I'm here to save Christmas from the imposter.'

'That's what I'm here to do! Let's help each other,' Juliet asked, her eyes pleading for the dark figure to say yes.

'OK. Why not? Just don't get in my way. I need you to do exactly as I say, when I say it. It should make things easier, with another pair of hands,' said Zappy.

Juliet peered out at the front of the sleigh. It was a bright ruby red and inside was no different. Running her hands over the paintwork, it felt thick and glossy. None of the kids at school were going to believe her when she told them about it!

As her eyes got accustomed to the dark, she could take in more details about Zappy. Zappy looked exactly the same size as the elf she'd seen earlier.

But, Zappy was sat cross-legged, with her back to the front of the sleigh and, laying across her legs, was what looked like a large toy gun.

Juliet's curiosity got the better of her. She had to know who this elf was and what it was that she was carrying.

'Excuse me,' said Juliet, in her most polite voice.

'What?' snapped the elf.

'Am I right in thinking that you, er …. are an elf?' she spoke with a low voice, rather embarrassed to have to ask.

'Yes, what of it?' retorted the elf.

'You look very similar to the elf sitting at the front of the sleigh, that's all.'

'Humph,' bristled the disgruntled elf.

'Also,' Juliet continued bravely on, 'what is that strange looking gun thing on your lap?'

The elf brightened up a little. She was obviously proud of her creation. 'This is my Christmas blaster! I designed and built it myself. Do you see these dials on the side?'

One of her fingers pointed to a large black dial on the side of the blaster. 'If I press this, the gun shoots out different things. Each one is carefully created to sabotage the deliveries that the imposter is making.'

Suddenly, there was noise from the front of the sleigh, both the elf and the girl froze, as they heard muffled voices coming closer.

A sudden, sharp jerk and they were taking off. The sleigh started to sway gently, flying up and up into the night sky.

There was no going back now. They were flying through the air, and Juliet's cabin and her parents were disappearing fast behind them.

A moment of fear flashed through the her mind, but she pushed it out of her mind. This wasn't the time for nerves.

This was the time for courage. She had Christmas, and more importantly Santa, to save!

8

The Orphans at the Temple

Mrs Claus knew nothing about what was happening at the back of the sleigh.

'Phew!' panted Mrs Claus, 'that cabin was so warm and cosy, I nearly had to take my jacket off! Everything made of wood and beautifully carved. So lovely! Who are we visiting next? Let me take a look at the list.'

She pulled the list from her pocket. After she ticked off Juliet's name, she read out the name of their next stop. They were off to visit a group of orphans, living in a remote mountain temple. 'Japan here we come,' called Mrs Claus happily, to the reindeer.

She'd never been to Japan, but she had heard about the orphans' story. The monks had taken the children in, after they lost their parents in a terrible earthquake. They taught them everything they knew, clothed and fed them and had grown to love them.

Sadly, the monks couldn't afford much more than the bare essentials. The children only had a few toys to share between them. The monks couldn't even afford one small gift for the children this year.

What the monks didn't know was that Mrs Claus had been busy, personally making up a stocking full of small gifts for each child. She'd even got the elves to put together a special Christmas hamper for the monks, because they'd done so much for the children.

'Heading 42 degrees west, dropping to 50 feet... and touchdown!' squeaked Zippy as the sleigh did a perfect landing on the side of the snow-topped mountain, just outside the temple walls.

'Perfect landing, well done Zippy!' said Mrs Claus.

Mrs Claus had been practicing, and was now pretty confident with the jet pack.

The stealth pack, as she'd chosen to call it, started up silently. With the children's gifts tied securely, Mrs Claus rose slowly over the wall and into the temple courtyard.

She'd parked the sleigh outside, not wanting to disturb the peace of the temple and it's inhabitants.

She knew that the last thing that the monks were expecting was a visit from Santa this year. This made her even more excited about this delivery. She was so happy to be able to personally deliver the handmade stockings. As she had been making them, she'd imagined the children's happy faces on Christmas morning. A smile lit up her face in anticipation.

Mrs Claus glided softly through the temple, the stealth pack telling her where to go (it, of course, had built-in navigation). She soon found the orphans bedroom. Looking around the room, she counted nine beds. She gently deposited a stocking at the end of each bed and, just for fun, a red Santa hat for each child.

'This stealth pack is amazing! It makes me almost glad that I broke my ankle,', she thought.

She was seriously considering using the stealth pack next year, even when her ankle had healed. It would mean saying goodbye to the worry about treading on creaky floor boards or tripping over the wires for Christmas tree lights.

She decided she'd put the monks hamper in the kitchen. She wanted them to see it as soon as they woke up and went to make breakfast for the children.

Mrs Claus had never been to Japan before, so she was rather curious about everything. Looking around the temple, she could see it was a beautiful, ancient building, hundreds of years old.

Pondering why on earth these peaceful monks would need a dojo, Mrs Claus rose up slowly over the wall. It was time to head back to the sleigh. She was ready to continue her journey.

As she rose up over the wall, she really was *not* expecting the sight that met her eyes next.

9

The Unexpected Helpers

The reindeer were sat in a heap of tangled harnesses. The sleigh lay on its side, with presents spilling out onto what looked like snow.

It looked like there'd been an explosion!

'Don't come any closer!' yelled Zippy.

'What on earth has happened?' asked Mrs Claus.

'We were waiting for you. Then, out of nowhere, snow started coming out of the back of the sleigh. The reindeer panicked, bolted and now they are all tangled together.'

Mrs Claus watched as snow came pouring out and over everything surrounding the sleigh. It was cold up in the mountains, but there was only snow on the peaks, not here in the foothills. Mrs Claus and Zippy were puzzled, where had all the snow come from and how did it get there?

'If I get too close, I'll get caught in it too. What shall we do Mrs Claus?' asked Zippy.

Mrs Claus was at a loss. Her first delivery had gone so well. Now this had happened.

It felt like someone out there didn't want her to deliver these presents. Of course, that was a crazy thing to think. Why would anybody want to stop children receiving their Christmas presents?

'It must just be a coincidence,' thought Mrs Claus. 'Maybe this is some strange Japanese weather phenomenon. I'll have to ask Santa about it, when we get home. But for now, I'll just have to see if I can help my poor team with their harnesses.'

'Hold on there, I'll figure out a way to get you all out. I just need a moment to think,' she called out to the reindeer.

KAZOOMMMM!

'What on earth was that?' exclaimed Mrs Claus.

Something was flying through the air, trying to free the reindeer.

Astro shook his head free, which was worryingly close to Leaky's hind quarters. The yellow snow that Leaky had been creating since the snow had appeared, had been inching its way towards Astro. Astro was relieved, he could now raise his head out of the inevitable stream.

Mrs Claus looked wildly around her, trying to see who was helping them. But she couldn't see anyone, all she could see were the shadows cast by the temple walls.

'Show yourselves,' she called out. She knew that someone had come to help. Mrs Claus was curious to see who, or what, and where those flying discs had come from.

Suddenly, out from the shadows, seven shapes emerged and stood in a line. They bowed respectfully to Mrs Claus.

Ninjas! Mrs Claus couldn't believe her eyes. She had, of course read about them, but had never witnessed their stealth and skill before. The tallest of the ninjas stepped forward and spoke.

'Greetings Mrs Claus, you are most welcome here. You find us most unprepared for your arrival. We did not think that you would venture so far north. We did not put out the customary saki and sugar cookies. (Saki is a warming drink that adults like to enjoy in Japan and cookies, well, you know what cookies are). We humbly ask your forgiveness, venerable Mrs Claus.'

Mrs Claus flushed with the sincerity and humility of the tallest ninja.

It was beginning to dawn on her, exactly who her rescuers were. 'No apologies necessary, you have come to our rescue.' Said Mrs Claus 'I must ask, are you the orphans that I came to visit tonight?'

At that, the ninjas took of their face masks, revealing a line of young faces, beaming with happiness. They bowed again, in answer to her question.

Another of the ninjas stepped forward. 'Although we have started to free your team there is still work to be done.'

'Let us help you and the reindeer continue your journey.'

With that, the ninjas moved with great speed. They were able to release the reindeer, despite the piles of snow surrounding everything.

Next, they went back into the temple and came out with planks of wood, which they placed carefully over the strange snow, making bridges for each of the reindeer to walk to safety. The snow had made everything icy and slippery, so the oldest ninja walked across and led each one of the reindeer across the bridge.

Now that the reindeer were safe, the team got to work on the sleigh. With three ninjas on each side of the sleigh, they attached ropes and pulled it right side up, using the wooden planks to slide it to safety.

Quick as a flash they gathered all the fallen presents and placed them neatly back in the rescued sleigh.

Mrs Claus just stood there blinking. She thought she'd seen a thing or two at her home in the North Pole, but she'd never witnessed anything quite like this!

'Thank you, how can I ever repay you for your kindness?' asked Mrs Claus.

'Mrs Claus, it's us who are repaying you for your kindness,' said the tallest ninja, holding up his handmade stocking with a big smile on his face.

Mrs Claus breathed a sigh of relief.

If she'd known what was happening somewhere at the back of the sleigh, she might have felt rather differently.

10

The Imposter is Captured!

At the back of the sleigh it was a different story. Juliet had watched as Zappy used the Christmas blaster to shoot some sticky-looking snow at the reindeer and elf in front of them. The snow came out of the blaster, in waves. There was soon a mountain of the stuff.

Juliet didn't much like the look in Zappy's eyes. The little elf kept her finger on the trigger and was muttering repeatedly, 'This will show her.'

Juliet knew that she had to take out the imposter sooner rather than later. She thought she'd force her to tell her where they were keeping Santa. Maybe Zappy would help, by lending her the Christmas blaster?

What the two stowaways were not banking on was the reindeer getting into such a tangle and tipping the sleigh over. They'd ended up on top of each other in a heap, at the side of the sleigh.

'Get off!' whispered Zappy angrily, pushing Juliet away.

'Sorry Zappy,' Juliet whispered back. She scrambled up, only to fall back on top of Zappy when the sleigh righted itself.

'Grrrrr!' spat Zappy with a mouth full of curly hair. 'Right, it's time you made yourself useful. You grab the imposter and tie her up. Do you think you can handle this simple task?'

'I think so, but …'

'Good, whistle when you've got her.'

Juliet was not sure how she was supposed to overpower a fully grown woman. After all, she was only seven, nearly eight. She was strong for her age, but it was going to take a seriously good plan to capture the imposter.

No one was at the front of the sleigh, so she crept across the deck and looked over the slide. Then she had an idea!

A moment later she saw the imposter coming back to the sleigh. Now was her chance. She'd already decided what to do. She always kept a sling shot with her and she had an excellent aim. While the others were looking she took aim on her target.

TWANG!!

At that moment, it all went dark for Mrs Claus.

11

The Real Imposter

Mrs Claus woke up blinking her eyes with a throbbing pain in the middle of her forehead. What on earth had happened?

One minute she was hovering over from the sleigh to deliver more gifts and next she was lying on the floor of the temple.

Mrs Claus looked around. Standing behind her was an elf, and a young girl. The girl with long curly hair was wearing a reindeer onesie and looking very pleased with herself.

She caught a glimpse of Zippy, cowering in the background. Her hands were tied together behind her back. Instinctively, she began to wriggle her hands to free them.

'Who are you?' asked Mrs Claus, still in a daze from the pain in her head.

'I will be asking the questions here!' said Zappy.

'Imposter!' cried Juliet.

'Imposter? What are you talking about it?' said Mrs Claus, sounding confused. 'Let me go and we won't say any more about it. I'll let you ride in the sleigh and take you home.'

'Who are you and what have you done with Santa? ' asked Juliet.

'My dear, I think there's been some kind of mistake,' replied Mrs Claus. As she spoke and smiled, behind her back, she could sense that her hands were almost free.

All this arguing was upsetting the reindeer. Leena, who hadn't been feeling well, began to feel even more poorly.

'Doh Doh,' said Leena, quietly.

Then she began to shake, small shivers at first but soon her whole body was quivering like she had turned to the jelly in a Christmas trifle.

'I don't want to panic anybody,' said Mrs Claus with care, 'but I think there's about to be an explosion. I suggest that we move behind the sleigh.'

Everybody raced to shelter, except for Leena who was trembling from antler to toe. Oh, and Zappy.

'You won't trick me like that,' she said, standing her ground.

But the thing is, when a reindeer sneezes, it's best to be a long way away. Nobody has ever seen a reindeer sneeze, but that's because clever people know when it's time to hide.

Unfortunately, Zappy was not that clever. And that's how she became the first elf ever to experience a reindeer sneeze.

It wasn't pretty. Firstly, she was aware that the ground was beginning to shake as much as Leena. Then, the air disappeared as she took her final pre-sneeze breath in.

Zappy found herself sucked towards her. There was a moment of quiet, then a rush of outward air which lifted Zappy off her feet and banged her hard into the temple wall.

Now, reindeer snot travels faster than sound. It actually travels faster than a fighter jet, at least for a short while. So by the time a ginormous 'Aitchoo' reached Zappy's ears, she had already turned green. And hot. And sticky. From the top of her head, down to her toes.

There's another thing about reindeer snot that not many people know. It dries almost instantly. So, by the time her ears had stopped ringing, Zappy was already set solid. The only things she could move were her eyes and mouth.

Zippy ran over and stood staring at Zappy.

'Zappy, what were you doing?' she asked.

'You stole my job as chief engineer for Mrs Claus' deliveries today,' sobbed Zappy.

'So, that's what's going on.' Mrs Claus and the ninjas stepped (well Mrs Claus hovered) into the clearing. 'Zappy what do you think you were doing?'

Tears streamed down the elf's face. 'I worked so hard on your jet pack, I thought that you would choose me to be your chief engineer tonight' she sobbed

Then she continued her sad story. 'I thought that if you got hurt during the snowboarding tournament, you would need one of my inventions to help you deliver all the presents. I didn't want you to get too hurt, and I'd already designed the jet pack so you could make all the deliveries.'

Mrs Claus gasped. She couldn't believe that it was one of her own elves that had sabotaged her at the snowboarding tournament.

'I thought that you had the blue prints a bit too quickly Zappy' squeaked Zippy.

'But then *you* took all the credit for my hard work Zippy! Zappy pointed furiously at her sister.

Zippy looked at the ground, feeling rather sorry for herself.

'You know, poor Zappy looks pathetic, all green and sticky like that. Shouldn't we give her another chance?' said Mrs Claus.

Zappy tried to nod her head, but she couldn't.

'I've heard enough. You've both been silly and done something foolish. You both need to say sorry to each other.'

The head ninja took out a throwing star and it spun expertly into the dried snot holding Zappy firm. The metal star made a huge crack in the snot's crust and, as Zappy began to move, it crumbled around her.

Zippy and Zappy, the two sisters, fell crying into each other's arms, tears and snot running down their backs. Sometimes it gets messy when sisters fall out, and even messier when they make up again.

'I'm so sorry Mrs Claus, you got hurt badly because of what I had done and I nearly messed up the special deliveries for all those children. I just wanted you to pick me. I'm so sorry.'

'Thank you for saying that Zappy,' said Mrs Claus graciously. Turning to Juliet now 'I can see that you have got mixed up in all of this.'

'Where is Santa?' demanded Juliet.

'Why, my dear, he's out on the sleigh delivering presents. I'm Mrs Claus, Santa's wife. He asked me to help him deliver to some of the tricker places. Santa's not getting any younger and is happy to have a bit of help, now and then.'

'Who are you and how did you manage to climb aboard my sleigh?' she asked Juliet.

Juliet was dumbfounded, she didn't know what to say.

She had thought that Mrs Claus, Santa's wife, was an imposter!

She'd got everything wrong.

Juliet felt rather embarrassed and suddenly felt quite homesick. She wished she was tucked up in bed, safely at home.

'I'm so sorry Mrs Claus! I didn't know! I was in my treehouse waiting for Santa to come. Then I saw you and thought that something awful had happened to him!' she whispered.

'Oh, so you are Juliet, my first stop,' said Mrs Claus smiling, 'Don't cry, you were very brave to come aboard my sleigh and you thought that you were helping my husband. How can I possibly be cross about that?'

Juliet stopped crying and smiled.

'Can you answer one question for me?' asked Juliet

'Anything' replied Mrs Claus.

'Where did you find these ninjas from?'

'I didn't find them, they found me! These ninja's have saved me and they've rescued my reliable reindeer.'

At her words, the ninja's solemnly bowed low to Mrs Claus.

The tallest ninja stepped forwards once more to speak for the rest of the group.

'Most worthy Mrs Claus, you give us great honour by your words. Will you still like to step inside for refreshment, or do you now need to be on your way?'

'I would love to stay, but I fear we have lost too much time as it is,' said Mrs Claus

'If there is anything we can do to help, just say the word.'

'Hmm…' pondered Mrs Claus. 'Let me think for a moment.'

12

The Christmas Ninjas

The sleigh was packed, the two elves working together at the front, beside them Mrs Claus and Juliet in her reindeer onesie and a troupe of ninjas in the back.

The ninja's had swapped their black balaclavas for the red Santa hats they'd found on their beds. Tonight, for one night only, they were Christmas ninjas!

Mrs Claus's helpers! The sleigh took off and the stars got closer and the ground began to whoosh below them.

They flew near and far, they visited islands and boats and lonely huts in quiet valleys and mighty mountains. Juliet and the ninjas were a real help.

Juliet was the navigator, finding the quickest way to their next stop. As for the ninjas, they were well, ninjas. They all worked perfectly together like they had been doing it for years.

Mrs Claus jet pack worked perfectly, but they had lost so much time with events in the mountain temple. With Juliet and the ninjas by her side, they made up the time they had lost.

They delivered presents to tents, trains and cabins. They landed on snowy fields and in sandy deserts.

As they flew, Mrs Claus told Juliet about all the marvellous places they were flying over. She told her about her adventures delivering presents and she told her about life at the North Pole.

Juliet told Mrs Claus how much she longed to meet Santa.

And, finally, they laughed together about how Juliet had mistaken Mrs Claus for an imposter!

They went to so many different places that Juliet began to lose count. They visited the tropical island of Bali, buzzed low over elephants in Africa. They flew over Paris and the Eiffel tower, with all it's sparkling lights. They flew across green forests and over dark oceans.

The only thing that was the same in every place they stopped was that there would be a boy, or girl, or both, quietly sleeping, a happy smile of anticipation on their face.

Finally they got to their last stop. It was far up a mountain near a ski lift in the Rocky Mountains of America, which is one of the last places in the world to see Christmas morning. There was a wooden building there, lonely at the moment, although busy during the day time. In fact, it was a mountain café, and the owners had a small daughter.

Juliet took the girls present out of the sack and handed it to Mrs Claus.

'Let's do this one together, just me and you.' Said Mrs Claus looking at Juliet. The ninjas stayed respectfully with the sleigh.

The pair walked (and hovered) over to the cabin, Mrs Claus took out her magic key and opened the door. They crept up the stairs and into the girls bedroom, her stocking was laid out on her bed, partly filled with her parents presents, but plenty of room for the ones from Santa and Mrs Claus'.

As they made their way back to the sleigh Juliet was very quiet.

'Are you ok Juliet? You seem very thoughtful,' asked Mrs Claus.

'I'm alright Mrs Claus, but I'm just sad. Now that our last delivery is done, I have to go home. I have had the most amazing time tonight and I'm worried I won't remember it.'

'It's true that some of your memories of tonight will seem like they are from a dream,' replied Mrs Claus. It was part of the magic of Christmas. Children sometimes wake up during deliveries, but the Christmas magic means that they'll just remember the visit as a dream.

'I don't think this will be the last that you will be seeing of me. You and the ninjas did well. Even with my jet pack, I would have struggled this year without you.'

'What are you saying Mrs Claus?' asked Juliet, barely daring to breathe, in case she'd misunderstood.

'Even if I hadn't broken my ankle, I think I'd have struggled to make all the deliveries this year.

Next year, my special delivery list is going to be even longer. I'd love you, and the ninja's, to help to deliver the gifts to the children. Then, when we're finished, you can all come back to the Christmas party at the North Pole and meet Santa, before going home. What do you think?'

Juliet stared, speechless, at the smiling Mrs Claus.

13

Homeward Bound

The lights at the Christmas tree were still flashing in their multicolour brilliance outside Juliet's home. The reindeer set the sleigh smoothly in front of the tree. Mrs Claus felt sad to see Juliet go back home.

She and Santa had spent so many years preparing and giving toys to children, she had not actually spent much time with children. Tonight spending time with the ninjas and Juliet had been wonderful. Next year seemed a long time away until she would see her friends again.

Mrs Claus helped Juliet down from the sleigh. She let the little girl ride on her jet pack by standing on her unbroken foot and holding on tight to Mrs Claus's waist.

The glided silently into the house and Juliet snuggled into her normal bed in the back room of the cabin. Juliet's parents were sleeping soundly and hardly moved when Mrs Claus embraced Juliet for the last time, both of them swallowing tears, knowing it would be a full 365 days until they would see each other again. But grateful for the memories they shared together.

Mrs Claus left the cabin and wiped a solitary tear from her eye.

'What fortunate parents, Juliet has, to have such a brave and kind daughter.' Mrs Claus said quietly to herself.

'Are you alright Mrs Claus,' asked Zappy

'Yes thank you Zappy, what a wonderful adventure we have shared together! And now we have to get these orphans back to the temple before sun rise. It's going to be a push but I think we should make it in time.'

Before she knew it the wooden house was far behind them and the mountain range filled the sky.

When they touched down outside the temple gates as the sun peaked over the horizon, there was someone waiting for them! In fact there were a lot of someone's waiting for them. All of the monks from the temple were standing outside with looks of relief on their faces as they saw the orphan ninjas returned.

'Greetings, kind monks!' called Mrs Claus. 'I was hoping to get them back a little earlier, I'm so sorry! But they were so helpful with my deliveries tonight.'

The ninjas filed out of the sleigh and stood in front of the monks.

Mrs Claus hovered over to the head monk, who wore a yellow sash over his red robe.

'Mrs Claus,' said the monk, bowing respectfully

'Sir, can we have a word or two?' Mrs Claus and the monk walked off a short distance away and spoke for a few minutes before they returned.

Mrs Claus turned to the children and said nervously, 'My Christmas ninjas! I have asked the head monk and he has agreed. If you would like to come with me to deliver the children's presents next year, Santa and I could really use your help! We'd love you to come and visit us at the North Pole, if you'd like to'

'My children, my brothers and I would be happy, if you wish to go,' said the head monk.

The children looked excitedly at each other and the ninja leader stepped forward.

'Blessed monks, and Mrs Claus, it would be an honor to help you next year. We will work on honing our ninja skills every day, between now and Christmas Eve.'

The sun was well up before the orphans were tucked in their beds, for a short nap, before breakfast.

They waved goodbye to Mrs Claus, who waved back excitedly from the back of the sleigh.

Every heart was full of excitement and anticipation for their next Christmas adventure.

14

Christmas Morning

Back at the North Pole, Mrs Claus finally touched down back at home. Santa looked very happy to see his wife back safely.

'Am I glad to see you! I was about to send the search elves out when I saw that you hadn't got back home after sunrise.' Relief visibly pouring off Santa's brow.

'I'm so sorry my love, we had a few problems this year, but all sorted now.'

Santa beamed, he was happy to have Mrs Claus home. Maybe one Christmas, she would have a normal delivery run.

Somewhere in the middle of a forest, an excited girl was waking up on Christmas morning.

'Wake up Mum, wake up Dad. It's Christmas Day!' Juliet shook her parents awake. Then she climbed up on the bed and started to jump up and down.

'Good morning Juliet. I see you've woken up bright and early!' said dad.

'Did you see Santa, when you were in your treehouse, Juliet?' asked her mum.

'No, I didn't' said Juliet. Once again, she was telling the truth, just not the whole truth. She was dreaming about next Christmas and remembering what Mrs Claus had promised her.

'Oh well, never mind, maybe next year,' said dad, reaching out his arms and pulling her towards him for a hug.

'Juliet, why is there snow on your boots?' asked mum. It had been a cold, but snow-free winter, so far this year.

'I'm not really sure how to explain …..' replied Juliet.

Juliet smiled to herself, the kind of smile you smile, when you know a secret that no-one else knows.

THE END

15

One More Thing

If you've enjoyed this book, please consider leaving a rating or review.

You might also be interested to listen to another Christmas book for children by the Publisher:

A Christmas Surprise - a refreshing look at the nativity story at the real Christmas story by those who saw it .

Four short stories look on at the story of the birth of baby Jesus as seen by the donkey in the stable, the shepherds on a hillside, the star gazing down on the little town of Bethlehem and the baby's mother, Mary.